DRAGON TALES

Book V

Dragons in Snow

This is fe Rio

Judy Haynes.

This is the fifth of the Dragon Tales Chronicles.
Already published:
Dragon Tales Book I: Quest for a Cave
Dragon Tales Book II: Quest for a Friend
Dragon Tales Book III: Quest for Adventure
Dragon Tales Book IV: The Runaway
The Dragon Tales Colouring Book
Coming soon:
Dragon Tales Book VI: The Dragons' Call

DRAGON TALES

BOOK V

Dragons in Snow

by

Judy Hayman

illustrated by

Caroline Wolfe Murray

Practical Inspiration
PUBLISHING

First published in Great Britain by Practical Inspiration Publishing, 2016

© Judy Hayman 2016
All illustrations by Caroline Wolfe Murray
The moral rights of the author and illustrator have been asserted.

ISBN (print): 978-1-910056-42-4
ISBN (ebook): 978-1-910056-43-1

This one is for Kate, Martin and Rachel, in memory
of snowy winters past.
J.L.H.

For Bryony.
C.W.M.

What young readers say about the Dragon Tales books

'I like that the dragons go on adventures and have so much fun, and I love Ben McIlwhinnie. Emily's my favourite dragon because she loves books like I do.' - *Catherine, Hampshire*

'Thank you for the dragon books. My favourite is *Quest for a Friend* because I find Desmond really entertaining, and I think the baby is really cool.' - *Jessica, Guildford, Surrey*

'I love the Bonxie bird in *Quest for Adventure.* He is really funny. I love his Scottish words and really laughed when he was telling the other birds to leave Des alone in Ice Land, especially when he told them not to poo on Des.' - *Kirstyn, Clackmannanshire*

'I like Tom because he is really funny. I am reading Book 4 and enjoying the dragons trying to find Ollie and flying to different places.' - *Fraser, Southall, Notts*

'I love how the books get more and more exciting. Also I like the way the books are worded. I like the way the dragons show their feelings because they are like people. My favourite is Des, because he takes all sorts of risks.' - *Aly, Haddington, East Lothian*

My favourite character is Tom, and I liked the bit where he did a head-stand in the water, and how he sits on Ben McIlwhinnie's ear. - *Matthew, Staveley, Derbyshire*

'I love the way that all of the dragons in *Quest for a Cave* are shades of blue. And it is funny when Emily thought the JCB digger was a yellow dragon! - *Jarosan, Yateley, Hants*

'*Quest for a Cave* was a fun childhood read with an interesting twist. I am looking forward to the next books.' 'Very enjoyable! I liked the mountain giant best.' - *Kayla and Ailsa, Musselburgh, East Lothian*

'I really enjoyed *Dragon Tales* because I felt like I was there. I like drawing pictures of Tom playing on the mountain giant's ear.' - *Skye, Edinburgh*

'Our favourite character is Lily, because she is a baby dragon with a lot of temper. She is the classic bossy little sister!' - *Stella and Sarah, Haydon Bridge, Northumberland*

'We liked the part in Book 4 where Georgie pulled Tom's spiky tail because he wanted to play.' - *Lucy and Andrew, Edinburgh*

'I like dragons, so I really like all your books. My sisters Skyla and Milly loved hearing what dragons like to eat and looking at Elise's pictures. My favourite book is *The Runaway*, because Ollie ends up getting found by people and now they are looking for all the dragons. It makes it exciting to keep reading.' - *Kaleb, Herekino, New Zealand*

Table of contents

Chapter 1

Goodbye until Spring!

Emily the Dragon sat on the landing branch of the tree house that she had built so happily with Tom, Alice and Ollie earlier in the summer. It had been the best summer ever, especially their seaside adventure with Des. But now every bit of her was drooping miserably: wings, ears, tail, talons. Two tears slithered down her scales and dripped down her neck. Even her spikes felt limp. She couldn't even manage a final wave as the tiny flying shapes of her friends disappeared into the distance on their way south for the winter.

A silence fell.

Down below, her Mum, Dad and younger brother Tom had been waving and shouting goodbye, while baby Lily bounced and huffed in excitement, not understanding what all the fuss was about. But now they all turned to look up at the sad heap of Emily, just visible in the gathering dusk. She didn't want to talk to anybody. She pushed her way through the bracken doorway and buried herself as deep as she could into the pile of left-over heather on the floor.

"Leave her alone for a while," Gwen said to Tom, who was about to fly up to the branch. "She'll cheer up! Why don't you help us clear up the last bits of their camp and then we can go home."

"It looks clear enough to me," said Tom, miserably. He wasn't as upset as Emily, but he wasn't looking forward to a winter without the excitements that Ollie and Des could provide.

"We mustn't leave any trace, remember?" said Duncan. "You never know when Humans might come snooping. You rough up that flattened grass with your tail while we pack up these things to store in the cave." Tom set to work, while his father collected all the remaining firewood from the camp and tied a neat bundle with an ivy strand.

When they had finished, there was still no sign of Emily.

"You go on, and take Lily," Gwen said. "Get the fire going and supper ready. It's going to be a cold night." She gathered the remaining heather from the beds in the camp and flew to the landing branch with it. She sighed sympathetically as she peered in at the quivering heap on the floor, and wondered how she could cheer her daughter up. It wasn't going to be easy!

Buried in her heather, and still sobbing, Emily was remembering the last few weeks with Alice and Ollie. After the dramatic rescue of Ollie from the Humans' cage, she and Alice, with Ollie and their Dads, had flown back home to a wonderful welcome. She pictured Tom as she had seen him dancing and cheering on top of Ben McIlwhinnie's bald head when they flew in, and then Ellen hugging her son – who didn't seem to mind, to Emily's surprise – and Georgie and Lily getting under everybody's claws. And how they took turns to tell the tale of the search and rescue and the help the Hawks and Owls had given, while they devoured the hot supper that had been waiting for them. And how proud she and Alice had been as their Dads told about the important parts they had played in the whole adventure. And how they all fell silent and huddled a little closer together round the fire as Ollie had told the story of how he had been captured and imprisoned. She still shuddered when she remembered that awful cage and the sight of a miserable and frightened Ollie inside it. It had taken seven of them to huff a hole in the wire big enough for him to escape.

Then, ten days later, there had been the excitement of Des returning, as he had promised, to tell how he had escorted Old George and Aunt Angelica to her famous Castle, and had a good snoop round before making the journey back. "It's a pretty good place she's found," he had reported. "OK, nearer to Human settlements, but well hidden. There's a high fence all round, and pretty dense woodland. She's got good stores of food and plenty of room."

So sadly everything had been decided. Ellen, Oliver and the children would fly south to spend the winter in the castle, and Des would go too, to show them the way, and perhaps to stay himself during the worst of the weather. He comforted Alice and Ollie with the thought that there was room enough for them to keep well out of Angie's way, and even Ollie had to agree that it was the only thing to do. His adventure, when he had narrowly escaped a zoo, seemed to have made him a good deal more sensible, though both Alice and Emily wondered if it would last.

But none of these memories helped Emily now. There had been two happy weeks before they left, the departure delayed by three days of high wind which had stripped the last of the leaves and warned of bad weather to come. The children had enjoyed the wind, laughing and tumbling in the air, playing complicated chasing games, but finally, yesterday, it had dropped. The air turned colder, and Des insisted it was time to go.

As usual, they had set off in the gloaming to fly at night and hide by day, and now that they had gone, Emily had to face a lonely winter.

Sniffing, she realised that her mother had come in quietly and was sitting on the floor beside her heap of heather.

"I know, Emily, it's hard for you and Tom! You've had a lovely summer, and a lot of excitement. But it won't be as bad as you think. They've promised to come back in the spring. And Tom's growing up. He was a lot more sensible while you were away looking for Ollie, even though he was disappointed not to go with you. He'll miss Ollie and Alice as well. You'll manage, with him, and Lily, and your books. Didn't you swap one with Alice before she left? So that's a new story you have! Come on, the supper will be burning."

Emily knew she couldn't stay buried forever. Slowly she emerged, damp, miserable and covered in bits. Her mother smiled sympathetically. "Let's go home," she said, holding out a talon.

Emily sighed deeply. "I suppose I am a bit hungry..." she admitted. They flew back to the cave together.

Mum was right when she said that Tom was growing up, Emily thought, as she ate her crow and toadstool hotpot. In the past he would have laughed at her for crying, but this time he didn't and after the hotpot was finished, he even offered her the last dried rosehip and helped to clear up without complaining. When they had finished, they sat for a while in the firelight, and the stars shone bright and clear. The moon was a thin crescent low on the horizon.

"It's a perfect night for their flight," said Gwen, coming out after putting Lily to bed and speaking of their absent friends for the first time. "I hope they manage to find a good safe spot to hide during the day tomorrow."

"Des knows all the good places," said Duncan. "They'll be fine. He'll find them a hidden spot where they can sleep. I wonder if he'll stay with them all winter."

"Des never stays anywhere for long," said Tom. "Perhaps he'll come back here."

"No, he won't do that. He knows we've only just enough space and food to keep the five of us going until the spring. What we must do now is make sure we're ready for the winter ourselves. You two will have plenty to keep you occupied, don't worry. Firewood and foraging tomorrow! No time to brood."

"OK," said Tom, before Emily could reply. "Bags I do berries."

"No chance. You always eat as many as you save!" his Dad teased him.

Emily began to feel better. Perhaps her mother was right about Tom. She heaved a deep sigh, her huff smoky in the cold air. "I think I'll go to bed and read Alice's book," she said. "Come on, Tom, it's getting cold out here."

Their parents smiled at each other as the young dragons disappeared.

"They'll be all right," said Gwen.

"And I reckon the others got away just in time," said Duncan thoughtfully. "There's going to be a frost tonight. Winter's here!"

"And earlier than usual! I think these last foraging days might be important, if our food's to last. Emily and Tom have bigger appetites these days, and we used up such a lot of food when the others came for meals."

"It might be time to try that roots idea that Oliver told me about," said Duncan thoughtfully as he banked up the fire with turf to keep it burning gently until morning.

His wife snorted. "I don't think a bit of digging will cheer the kids up. Better think of something more exciting if we're to survive the winter!"

Chapter 2

Foraging

Emily woke late the next morning and crawled out of her heather wondering why it was so quiet in the cave. She was relieved to see that her porridge was keeping warm on the fire, so she hadn't been forgotten, even though there was no sign of the rest of the family. It was a still, cold morning; the sun had not yet risen, and the hillside below the cave was white with frost. The stream sounded unusually loud in the frosty air. She huddled closer to the fire as she ate her porridge.

"Good, you're awake at last!" said a voice from behind, making her jump, and there was Gwen, with Lily riding on her back. "Lily got herself all over porridge this morning. She needed a good wash!"

Lily giggled. "'Tikky!" she said. "You certainly were!" her mother agreed, putting her down.

"Where're Dad and Tom?"

"They went down to the loch. Some idea that Duncan had. They said they wouldn't be long. I'll put some water on for tea when they come back. Do you want the rest of this porridge?"

"Yes please!" said Emily. Her mother passed it over, thinking again that her children's appetites were growing far too fast. They needed more food! For some reason there had been fewer rabbits on the hills this summer, and they had to be careful not to take too many fish from the otters' loch. This early frost was bad luck; it would have driven all the snails into hiding. She went into the cave for some nettles, feeling rather worried. Their pile of wild oats was getting smaller too.

As Emily finished her breakfast, she spotted Tom and her father flying back, and shouted a greeting. Lily danced up and down, waving. Gwen came out to make the tea.

"Any luck?" she asked.

Duncan poured mugs of tea and sat down near the fire. "Show them, Tom."

Tom opened his front claws and showed them a collection of small greyish-white roots.

"Yuk, what on earth are they?" Emily wrinkled her nose, but Gwen looked delighted.

"Des was right!" she said.

"What are you talking about?" said Emily, beginning to feel annoyed. She didn't like the feeling that she was the only one who didn't know about a secret, especially if Des was involved.

Duncan finished his tea in a noisy gulp, and decided to explain. "Remember that big round root that Des brought back from the castle? He said it was called a 'tattie' and was food that Humans cook."

"We roasted it in the fire," Emily remembered. "It was good! But these aren't tatties!"

"No chance of finding tatties round here. At that castle they're nearer Human places, and Des said he went foraging at night and dug some up on the edge of a field. Risky of course, but you know Des! Before he left he told me that he had heard about some wild roots like tatties from an old Traveller. Burdock's one plant that has good roots, and that plant with silvery leaves and wee yellow flowers that grows all over. Well, we found a patch of that this morning, and dug some up. He was right!"

Gwen was looking thoughtful. "I don't know what they'd taste like roasted, and we might lose them in a fire – they're so small. But we could add them to stew, to make it more filling. Can we get some more?"

"Lots, if we all dig. It would be easier without this frost, but the sun's coming up, so the ground might melt a bit. Let's not waste the daylight."

Tom proudly led the way down the valley a few minutes later. The patch of Silverweed was in one of the open glades that dotted the woodland not far from the loch. There were areas of scraped earth where Duncan and Tom had been busy earlier, but they set to work, digging into the frosty ground with their sharp talons and loosening the earth round the roots. It was quite hard work and the children were given the task of collecting the roots that were unearthed and piling them on the two square cloths that Ellen had given to Gwen as a goodbye present. The other family had collected quite a lot of useful Human items on their travels; if you held the cloth by its four corners it made a good bag for carrying the roots back to the cave. Even Lily trotted to and fro carrying one small root at a time.

As the sun rose higher the ground became easier to dig, but the dragons got a good deal more grubby in the process. When Lily tripped and fell with a loud wail in the muddiest patch, Gwen called a halt.

"We can't put much more in the bags without losing them on the way home," she said. "I'll take them back to the cave with Lily, clean her up and make the broth. You two have a break. See if you can find any more of the plant on the way to the loch. And have a wash while you're there!"

"I'll carry on," said Duncan. "Don't want to waste a good digging day. See you later."

Tom and Emily had quite enjoyed digging. It was fun clawing up the earth and finding the white hidden roots. And they had found a lot, in a very short time. "Good for Des! He really is brilliant!" Emily said as they set off towards the loch.

"Pity they're no good raw," said Tom, who had tasted one and spat it out in disgust. "I could do with a snack right now."

"Well, you're in luck," said Emily, pointing ahead. "Beech nuts!"

There was a lot of open beech-mast on the ground around the beech tree, and they crunched happily. Then Tom flew up to the branches, and found a lot more nuts still attached to the branches. "We'd better remember where this is!" he called down. "These would be easier to collect than roots, and nicer too."

"It will make Mum happier," said Emily as they set off towards the loch. "I think she's really worried that our food won't last the winter. We ate such a lot while the others were here!"

Tom didn't want to think about their absent friends, so he ran ahead to the loch shore, hoping to see the otters. There was no sign of them, but after a minute or two of gazing over the surface of the water they spotted two round heads, and suddenly Wattie and Lottie were shooting up to the shore and climbing onto their usual rock, shaking the water from their thick coats.

"Wha've ye bin daein'?" said Lottie, looking at the muddy snouts and talons of the two dragons.

"Digging roots."

"Wha' fer?"

"We cook and eat them," Emily explained, washing the mud off in the loch and shivering in the cold water. Wattie pulled a face. "Sounds mingin'!" he said. "Comin' fer a swim?" Tom agreed, took a deep breath and dived in, but Emily shook her head.

"Aye, water's a bit nippy," Lottie agreed, climbing off the rock and joining Emily on the shore. "Gettin' icy further roond. Dad says we're in fer a bad winter. Loch micht freeze ri' o'er."

She trotted away round the shore, and showed Emily a thin skin of ice stretching across a shallow bay. Reeds stuck stiffly through the ice, each rimmed with frost. The sun hadn't reached this part of the loch and it was cold in the shade.

"How will you manage to fish if it does freeze over?"

"Nae idea. Dad'll ken wha' tae dae. We'll no' starve. He sez the loch froze richt o'er when he was oor age, an' they a' had a great time slidin' o'er the ice. Mum sez we c'n coorie doon 'n' sleep a lot o' the time, so we dinnae get as hungry in the winter."

Emily put one foot on the ice, but it cracked and shifted under her.

"Not strong enough yet," she said. "It will be fun when it is, though. We'd better get back to Dad. TOM!" she shouted as she saw him surface further out in the loch. He waved and started back to the shore. Emily went to meet him, followed by Lottie. He scrambled out, carrying a medium-sized fish in one talon.

"Did you catch that?" she asked, impressed.

"No, Wattie did," Tom admitted. "He gave it to me. Said they've caught lots today." They shouted thanks to the young otters, waved, and set off back through the wood. On the way back, Emily spotted another patch of Silverweed, and noted it for later. It wasn't far from the beech tree.

"Mum Huffed that lunch is ready," said Duncan as they came close to his diggings. He had made quite a pile of new roots for them to collect later, and was covered in mud. "You fly on, and I'll have a quick wash and catch you up. Nice fish, Tom! Did you catch it?" He set off without waiting for Tom's reply.

"Come on, let's fly fast. You're shivering," said Emily, setting off up the hill. Tom shook water off his wings and followed, looking forward to a hot meal by the fire.

Gwen had chopped some of their roots and added a good clawful to the beetle broth simmering on the fire. There wasn't much flavour to them, but they certainly added bulk and filled them up. She was looking a good deal happier. She was delighted with Tom's fish, which she said they could have for supper, and even more pleased to hear about the tree full of beech nuts.

"I think we should go down this afternoon as well," she said as Duncan, clean again, flew down to join them. "You never know what the weather will be like tomorrow."

"Lottie's Dad says it's going to be a hard winter. There's ice on the loch already," Emily reported.

"Then we'd better not waste a good foraging day," Duncan agreed.

They collected their bags and flew back down as soon as the meal was finished. Gwen made a nest in the grass under the beech tree, and persuaded Lily to climb inside. "Coorie doon, Lily!" Emily said. "That's what Lottie says. I think it means snuggle down," she added for her mother's benefit as they tiptoed away.

With Lily asleep, the others found foraging much easier. Duncan bagged up his pile of roots and sent Tom back to the cave with them, while he started on the digging. Tom happily joined him when he returned with the empty bag. Gwen and Emily flew up to the spreading branches of the beech tree, tied their cloth between twigs, and started to fill it with nuts. The sun filtering through the branches felt surprisingly warm on their scales.

"Are you sure this is the start of winter?" Emily asked. "I'm lovely and warm."

"That's because there's no wind," said Gwen, dropping a clawful of nuts into the cloth. "It'll be cold again when the sun goes down. The frost hasn't melted in that patch of shade down there."

"Are we really going to be short of food?"

"I don't think so," Gwen didn't sound too sure, "but it's as well to be as prepared as we can. The Otter is probably right about the winter being a hard one. He'll know the signs if he's lived here all his life. Frosty days like this are all right, but too much snow can be a problem. Food will certainly be hard to find, so we need our stores. I'd hate you and Tom to go hungry."

"Tom would get really grumpy!" Emily agreed.

"He wouldn't be the only one! Can you keep an eye on Lily while I take these back to the cave?"

Emily agreed and as there was no point in collecting more nuts until the bag was brought back, she flew to the topmost branch of the tree and perched, swaying gently. From there, she could see Tom and Dad still digging in the wood. Looking south over the loch she saw all four otters rolling and playing in the deep water and watched a pair of small deer tread warily to the edge of the loch for a drink before disappearing back into the trees. Two eagles, high in the pale sky, circled lazily. How would they all manage in a hard winter? There were months of cold weather still to come...

A wail from the ground below the tree interrupted her thoughts. Lily was awake. That probably put an end to foraging for the day, Emily thought, gliding down to reassure her wee sister that she had not been abandoned.

As the sun sank lower the frost returned, and the night was even colder; but the dragons, snug in their heather beds, 'cooried doon' and slept in comfort.

Chapter 3

The Tail-Stane Game

For the next week, the weather stayed calm and bright, but very cold. The frost thickened, outlining every twig on the trees with white, and only melted briefly where the sun caught it. The ice round the edge of the loch hardened day by day. The mountain hares that lived on the higher slopes had turned white. The foraging continued, and the young dragons went to bed early and slept late. Emily didn't mind about this, because it was when they were sitting round the fire in the gloaming that she missed her friends the most. It was better to go inside and read in bed until she fell asleep.

Gwen had been right about the hibernating snails, but by the end of the week, the shelves in the main cave were better stocked with stores of roots and nuts to join the supplies of dried fruit, berries, beetles, slugs and fungi, and the remains of the sea-weed that the children had brought back from their seaside expedition in the summer. Duncan had set off early on a rook-and-crow hunt, and Gwen decided that it was time to give the children a day off.

"Go and see those young otters," she said, "but be careful of the ice. I don't suppose it will be frozen right across yet."

Tom and Emily took off together, and flew right over and around the loch to check before landing on their usual bit of bank. There was open water in the middle of the loch, but quite a wide area all round the edge was frozen. The otters came shooting up to the edge of the ice, climbed up and lolloped across to join them, sliding to a stop as they hit the bank.

"Ye'll no fall through on this bit," said Wattie. "Tek a run and slide on yer belly. Like this, ken." He demonstrated, sliding fast towards the edge and dropping into the water head first. He reappeared in seconds. "Hae a shot! S'great!" he called, climbing out again.

"If ye dinnae want tae fall in, dig yer claws in tae stop yersel'," advised Lottie, seeing Emily hesitate. Tom was already climbing onto the ice and preparing to run. He got speed up, then slid fast on his tummy, tail and wings held high, talons stretched sideways. As he got close to the open water, he obviously started to panic, dug his talons into the ice, spun round in a circle, skidded sideways and then disappeared over the edge in a tangle of wings and tail. Emily watched open-mouthed, wondering whether to rush to the rescue, but before she could move, Tom's head appeared and he climbed out, dripping and looking rather stunned. Wattie was rolling over and over, laughing. Emily decided that she was not going to bother with this particular game!

"It's safer roond the bay," Lottie said. "No sae guid fer slidin' fast like, 'cos o' the reeds, but it's no' bad. C'm on."

She led the way along the bank, past a thicket of bulrushes, until they came to the shore of the bay. Wattie and Tom ran along the ice by the shore and joined them. In the centre of the bay, a broad path of flattened reeds showed where the young otters had been sliding before the ice thickened on the main loch. Emily decided this was safe enough, and was soon skating along as happily as the others, adding twirls to her performance, while Tom just worked at sliding faster and faster, trying to beat the otters. There was plenty of room in the bay, without venturing near the open water.

Presently there was a flurry in the water, and the twins' dad heaved himself onto the ice and slid towards them. "Aye, freezin' grand!" he said, when he'd got his breath back. "Ah mind a braw wee game we played when Ah wiz a cub. Ah wilnae' be a minute." He disappeared behind the bulrushes, and reappeared a moment later with a sizeable flat pebble clutched in one paw. He placed it in the middle of a smooth patch of ice and they all gathered round gazing at it.

"Richt, this is the Stane and ye've all got tails! This is wha' ye dae! Oot th' way..." He took a wide swipe with his powerful tail, and the stane skittered away over the ice. "Richt, aefter it!" The four of them ran, slipping and sliding, towards the stane. Lottie reached it first, swiped it with her tail towards Tom, who missed it. Emily, who was nearest, swung her tail as hard as she could and the stane shot across the ice towards open water. Wattie caught it before it fell in, and sent it shooting back.

Soon all five of them were passing the stane between them, slipping and sliding, rolling over, shoving each other out of the way. They were shouting and laughing so loudly that nobody noticed Duncan, standing on the bank, watching in amazement. Tom was the first to spot him.

"Hi, Dad!" he yelled. "Come and play. This is great!" He swiped the stane furiously and fell over. Wattie sent it shooting into the reeds and the three otters disappeared after it. Emily and Tom slid towards their dad.

"I finished the rook hunt and came for a quick dip to get rid of the feathers," Duncan was saying as the otters trotted over, dribbling the stane between them as they came. It was true – he did have rather a lot of tattered black feathers clinging to his scales and spikes.

"Comin' tae join us, like? If thiz three o' ye, we can play otters v. dragons. This is how ye dae it, ken." He demonstrated the side-swipe of the tail and the young otters galloped off to retrieve the stane. Duncan looked tempted.

"Right. You're on. Come on, you two!"

Soon there was a furious game in progress, the stane flying to and fro, getting caught in the reeds and once disappearing into the water, until the twins' dad dived in and retrieved it. They stopped for a breather, and had just changed sides, when the twins' mother appeared from the loch edge and came to join them. "Yez niver said ye wuz playin' on the ice!" she said indignantly, demonstrating a powerful and accurate tail-swipe.

"Not fair, four against three!" Tom protested, realising that this new player was particularly skilled.

"We need Mum," said Emily. "Shall I fly up and get her?"

"No need," said Duncan, pointing upwards, and they all saw Gwen gliding down to the bank, carrying Lily.

"Whatever are you doing? I could hear you right up the hill!"

"Come on, Mum – we need you. This is what you do..." Emily demonstrated.

"What about Lily?"

"She can sit here and watch, can't you, Lily?" said Duncan, skating fast over the ice with a shrieking Lily on his back, and placing her gently on a flat rock in a thicket of reeds.

"No!" said Lily. "'gen!" She held up her wings for another slide. Her father sighed. "One more, then you stay here and watch the game," he said, noticing that Gwen was having a Tail-Stane lesson on the opposite side of the ice.

With eight long tails swiping wildly, the area of ice in the bay seemed smaller, and there were a lot more collisions. Lily began by dancing and huffing in excitement but then she got bored and sat hunched up, looking grumpy. When Emily saw her wrap her wings over her eyes, she sighed and pointed. "Lily's in a huff," she said. Lily saw her looking, and shuffled round until her back was to them. Gwen sighed.

"Pity! I was just getting the hang of it," she said. "I suppose I'd better take her back. You two must be hungry – and Duncan, you're still covered in feathers!"

"See yez later, aye?" Wattie said.

"It'll be better when the loch's frozen richt o'er, though it meks the fishin' tricky," said the twins' dad.

"We'll likely head off tae the big river fer a while," added his wife. "Thiz always something ye c'n find tae eat in a river, even if it's no' as guid as oor fish. We'll be back when thiz a thaw, mind. This's a braw loch, ken. We dinnae want ither otters findin' it."

Lottie saw Emily and Tom looking downcast. "Dinnae fash, we'll no' be goin' yet," she said. "See yez the morn, richt?"

"Right!" said Emily, and she and Tom prepared to fly home. Duncan had dived into the loch, saying he would be back at the cave soon after them.

"Even the otters are leaving," said Emily sadly as they flew up the hill.

"Ollie would have loved that Tail-Stane game. Des too."

"And Alice! She'd have been really good on our team. I wish they were still here."

30

"It's not fair!" said Tom. "Why can't we go somewhere new like all the others? There'll be no one to have fun with until the spring."

Gwen was surprised by their downcast faces when they arrived at the cave a few minutes later. She had expected a pair of cheerful young dragons after the riotous time on the ice, but they both disappeared into the cave, saying nothing. "What's the matter with them?" she asked Duncan when he landed, damp but feather-free, a few minutes later.

"I expect it's because the otters might be leaving. They go wandering further afield looking for food if the loch freezes. That's probably reminded them how much they're missing their friends."

"We all are. I wish I knew how they're getting on. I'd love to get in touch on the Gloaming Huff, but they'll be out of range."

"We could take the kids on a longer foraging expedition, I suppose, while this weather holds," Duncan said thoughtfully.

"I think they're a bit sick of foraging," said his wife. "I know I am! Let's hope the otters stay for a while longer. A few more Tail-Stane games should cheer them up. But it's going to be a long winter!"

Chapter 4

Winter Closes In

For the next few days Tail-Stane matches were all the rage for the youngsters, and as the loch froze more and more, the play became wilder and faster. They left the reedy bay, and on the open ice the stane and the players slid faster. They had spent some time collecting a pile of suitable smooth flat stones, as they lost so many over the edge of the ice. Tom developed a new way of hitting the stane, by hovering just above the ice and clouting it with the end of his tail, to loud applause from all four otters. A stane hit that way went flying in unpredictable directions, which made the games more interesting, even though it disappeared into the water more regularly.

The otters hadn't yet left for the river, and spent a lot of time fishing as the ice crept nightly towards

the centre of the loch. Their fishing was so success-
ful that they sometimes shared their catches with the
dragon family, to Gwen's relief. She was a little tired
of Emily complaining that rooks and crows weren't
nearly as nice as the pigeons they had eaten on the
rescue expedition.

"Aren't you afraid you might be seen by Humans
near the big river?" she asked the otters during one of
their rests in the middle of a particularly strenuous
game.

"Naw!" said the twins' dad. "We hide up when
they're aroond. Ef they dae spot us, they get all excited like, but they niver try and nab us. Wudnae stand
a chance onyways. They cannae swim."

"An auld otter yince telt me they used to hunt us
w' dugs," added his wife. "Tha' cud've bin nasty, but it
doesnae happen th' noo."

"Sgin'tae be great," added Wattie happily. "Lottie
n' me've niver been oota this glen afore."

"When're we gaein', Da?" Lottie asked.

"Soon, afore th' snow staerts. Easier travellin' when
the groonds a' frozen."

"I wish you weren't going," Tom sighed. "It's going to be so boring with just Em." Emily was feeling too depressed to clout him with a wing, as she usually did.

"Why no' come tae?" asked Lottie. "Dragons c'n fly as faest's we c'n run."

"I asked Dad if we could," Emily said, "but he said no. It's because we mustn't be seen. If Humans spot an otter, that's OK, because they know about otters. They think dragons don't exist, remember? You know how all the grown-ups go on about it."

Tom snorted. "Not Des! He doesn't seem to mind being spotted. Sometimes I think he WANTS to be found, to see what will happen."

"Tha' gret daftie!" the twins' dad said. Unlike his cubs, he had no time for Des, who had disturbed his fishing far too often. "Ye'd think he've learnt wha' Humans can dae aefter young Ollie wuz ta'en. Want anither geme?"

"Girls v boys?" said Emily, who had learnt that the twins' mother was by far the best player. Sure enough, they won, and she felt more cheerful as they prepared to fly back to the cave. Tom was cheerful too, despite his defeat. He was enjoying all the applause for his new stane technique.

"Where's Dad?" he asked when they arrived.

"He thought he'd risk a fly right down the glen," said Gwen. "I think he's hoping to find a few pigeons. He's fed up with your complaints! I hope he won't be much longer – it'll be dark soon."

"I'll go up to Ben's head to see if he's coming," said Tom, flying off before anyone could object. He was gone a while, and Emily helped herself to some nettle tea to warm up while she told Gwen about the game, and Lottie's suggestion that they should go to the big river with them. Her mother sighed.

"Emily, you know why we can't!" she said. "Remember what happened when you and Ollie were spotted at our old cave? It even got into Humans' newspapers! They wouldn't make a fuss about an otter family. We have to stay safe, and that means well hidden! Cheer up! Winter won't last forever." She gave her a sympathetic pat and went into the cave.

"Feels like forever!" Emily muttered, finishing her tea.

It was very late when Duncan arrived home, triumphantly carrying a large pheasant that he had found down the glen. "I think I heard Humans shooting in the distance," he said, dropping it and getting his breath back. "They must have missed this one. It was a goner when I found it. Good eating!"

"Nice change from crow!" said Tom, and was set to plucking the feathers off for being cheeky. Emily took the long tail feathers to decorate her private cave.

"Bit risky, Duncan," said Gwen quietly, while the children were busy.

"I know, but I flew low and kept a close eye out. Easier when I'm alone. I'll go back early tomorrow – there may be more lying around. We still need all we can find before we're reduced to roots and berries! I can just about cope with bored kids, but bored and *hungry*... " He shook his head in mock despair and went to help Tom.

Duncan had gone again by the time Emily and Tom emerged for a late breakfast the next morning. Tom was disappointed – he had wanted to go too – but the two of them set off for the loch as usual, looking forward to a return Tail-Stane match. To their dismay, there was no sign of the otters. They called, and even flew to the holt in the far bank where they knew the otters slept, but the only sign there had ever been an otter family there was some footprints in the frozen mud on the bank and fish bones on a nearby stone.

"They've gone!" Emily felt like bursting into tears.

"They wouldn't have gone without saying goodbye!" Tom argued.

"They wouldn't have bothered coming all the way up to the cave just to say goodbye," Emily argued. "We knew they were going. I just didn't think it would be today."

They returned to their bank and gazed sadly at the pile of spare stones, but were too dejected to play by themselves. "Might as well go back," said Tom, and Emily agreed.

Back at the cave their mother listened sympathet-ically to the tale of the missing otters. "Why don't you go down to your tree-house?" she suggested. "You haven't been for ages, and you promised the others you'd keep an eye on it. Bits might need mending, and you must make sure it's watertight in case we get snow."

"Suppose so," said Emily, without much enthusi-asm, and they took off to fly down to the wood beside the small loch. They found it had frozen right over, and they had a run-and-sliding race to the far end and back before flying to the tree-house, feeling a bit more cheerful.

When they got there, they discovered that the bracken doorway had blown away and there were some patches of ice on the floor where the rain had dripped in, and even a few icicles hanging from the roof. "We could put more moss in those holes in the roof," Emily said, and they flew to a nearby tree with a thick layer growing up its trunk, collected plen-ty and pushed it firmly into as many cracks as they could find.

After Emily had climbed inside and reported no more daylight showing through the roof, they turned their attention to the open doorway. Tom suggested they replace the bracken with flat fir branches, and they worked together, finding a few on the ground, and cutting more from the tree until the doorway was full and much more watertight. They filled in the windows too, and then stood back to admire their work, feeling pleased with themselves.

They were both on the landing branch, packing gorse twigs into the thinnest places of the new door, when Emily spotted Duncan flying through the trees towards them.

"Well done!" he said, inspecting their work. "I thought you'd need help, but you've managed fine. I think that should last the winter. Good job you came down today. Have you seen the sky?" They had been so absorbed in the work that they hadn't noticed that the wind was rising. For the last week of hard frost the air had been still and very cold, but suddenly they both realised that a change was happening. A strong wind was blowing from the north, and when they flew above the trees they saw a huge bank of dark grey cloud rising in that direction.

"That means snow, for certain," said Duncan. "I saw it coming on my way home, and came to fetch you. With this wind there could be a blizzard, and it's easy to get lost. Let's get going."

"Did you find another pheasant, Dad?" Tom asked hopefully as they started for home.

"No, but I bagged some pigeons to keep Emily happy," said Duncan. "Let's hope we can get them cooked before it starts to snow!"

They were just in time. The pigeons, threaded on sticks over the fire, were charring nicely when the first flakes of snow began to whirl in the air around them. They carried them inside the cave to eat. There was plenty to go round, and they finished with hot nettle tea and dried rowan berries as it grew dark. By this time the snow was falling thickly, the fire was hissing and dying and they decided that bed was the best place for all of them. Even Tom agreed that the snow would probably still be there in the morning as he took a final clawful of berries to eat in bed and disappeared into his private cave.

Emily wished she had her bats to talk to as she snuggled into bed, but they were hibernating and she hadn't seen them for weeks. Thinking to herself that perhaps bats had the right idea, she burrowed into her heather bed and lay for a long time, worrying. Had the otters reached the big river and found a place to shelter from the snow? Was it snowing at the castle? Was Des still there? Was Aunt Angelica driving them all mad? How would she and Tom get through the rest of the winter without fighting, especially if they were stuck in the cave; and would their food last if the snow went on and on... Finally she fell asleep from sheer exhaustion!

Chapter 5

Blizzards and Buzzards

Several days later Emily and Tom, who had remembered the fun they'd had playing in the snow in previous winters and looked forward to it, were wondering if it would *ever* stop. The first morning had been fun, waking to a white world, with only the black thread of the stream breaking the smooth sweep of the ground. The snow had fallen all night, but it stopped briefly in the morning, and they all went for a flight down the glen to marvel at the bright emptiness. The wind had scoured the loch clear of snow, but everywhere else was covered, and drifts were piling against the trees. Tracks left by deer in the night were filling up with blown snow.

On the way back, they stopped to gaze at Ben McIlwhinnie, their friendly Mountain Giant, sitting asleep, motionless against a grey sky. He was the only thing in the white landscape not covered with snow. "I thought he'd look like a snow giant," Emily exclaimed. "I was going to go and sweep it off his head for him when we got home!"

"I expect he's warm inside, and that melts the snow," said Gwen.

"It helps to keep our cave warmer too," said Duncan. "Don't worry about Ben – he's slept through worse than this over the centuries. Here comes another flurry. Let's get home."

They flew back to the cave, almost blinded by the heavy flakes that blew in their faces. Emily realised that it would be very easy to lose your way in a bad snowstorm, and was glad when they reached the cave and were able to scramble inside and warm up.

"Good thing the wind *is* coming from the North," Duncan said when Tom complained that the head-wind was making flying harder. "It's not blowing snow into the cave. We're sheltered by that gorse bush too. We'll be fine, even if it snows for weeks. We'll stay nice and snug and sit it out."

So for the next few days, they had done just that! The snow continued to pile up outside, and the children were not allowed to go far in the few short breaks between snowstorms. On the second afternoon they made a tummy-run down the hillside, and spent a happy hour sliding down faster and faster into the drift at the bottom, and then flying up to the top to start again. Their parents joined them, glad to get out of the cave. But as the sky darkened the snow started again, and by the next morning their run had disappeared under the drifts. And for the next few days the snow hardly stopped and the sun was never seen. The clouds were so low they seemed to be sitting on Ben's head.

Somehow their lovely roomy cave seemed to have shrunk, and as the days went by, Emily reckoned it was getting smaller and smaller! They could only light a tiny fire just inside the cave entrance, otherwise the cave filled with smoke. Drinks were heated up with huff, and they got very tired of cold food.

They all got bored and snappy. Emily read her books over and over, until she could almost recite them, and then tried writing a story of her own on the smooth bit of wall in her cave. She rubbed out the tree-house plans from the summer, found a bit of left-over white stone and set to work, but the wall space ran out long before she got to the exciting bits.

Then her mother persuaded her to read a book aloud for Tom and Lily, which kept them occupied for part of a morning, but Lily got bored and kept interrupting. Duncan tried to invent games, but there wasn't enough room for the boisterous ones Tom liked best. They tried singing and storytelling, but that made Emily nostalgic for her grandparents, remembering Grandad's amazing storytelling and Gran's songs round the fire on their trip to the seaside. It all seemed so long ago and she wondered miserably if it was snowing in Wales and how the Gramps were surviving in this long cold winter. Everyone she was fond of seemed very far away!

After a week, when both young dragons were ready to explode with boredom, there was an unexpected bit of excitement. Late one afternoon, a large brown buzzard appeared at the cave entrance. Dad sent out a warning huff, but to his surprise, the bird didn't fly away. Instead it came closer. A second bird was circling overhead.

"Dinna' fret. Friends o' Sukki's," he said in a harsh voice, rather breathlessly. "Go' a message frae a pal o' yours, name o' Des. Ken whae Ah mean?"

Lily had scampered away to hide, but the rest of the family crowded to the cave entrance. "You've come from Des?" said Duncan in amazement.

"Naw, naw, Ah've come frae Sukki. She flew north tae me, and A've come up here tae tell ye the news. O'er far fer her tae fly, ken."

"Are they all right?" Gwen asked.

"Aye, no sae bad. Bidin' safe in a gret heap o' ruins, Sukki telt me. Plenty food tae go roond. Seems Des was worried aboot yiz. Thiz snaw all o'er the land. Naebody's moving at a'. Deid birds 'n' beasts all o'er. Even thae pesky Humans cannae get aboot."

"Do you need something to eat after flying all that way?" Gwen sounded a bit worried.

"Na, na. Plenty drookit rabbits lyin' around. Ma mate'll pick yin up. Ah'm off fer a drink at yon wee burn. Back th' noo." He flew away and the dragons looked at one another in amazement.

"How on earth did Des get buzzards to fly this far to check up on us!" Duncan exclaimed.

"Des is just..."

"...brilliant. We know!" Tom interrupted. "Dad, why don't we fly off with that bird? If he can get so far, we could too. We could go and spend the winter with the others. I'm sick of staying here by ourselves. There's nothing to do!"

"Far too dangerous," Duncan said firmly. "Remember we can't fly in daylight like he can."

"But he said...." He got no further as the buzzard returned. "Steartin' tae snaw agin," he said cheerfully. "Wul roost here fer the nicht, and head south the morn. Wind'll blaw us alang nicely gaein hame! See yiz afor we heed aff." He disappeared towards the nearest tree, and they saw him settle on a branch, ruffling his feathers. His mate joined him. Then the falling snow hid them from sight.

Emily drew a long breath. "Wow, that was amazing!" she said.

"I'm so glad they're all right! I've been wondering...." Gwen said.

"I don't see why we can't go!" Tom carried on with his argument. "If there's no Humans out, like he said, we could fly in daylight. We've done it before. Old Ange said they had lots of room. Please!"

"NO!" said Duncan, sounding unusually firm. "It's far too dangerous flying in these conditions. We could get hopelessly lost in a blizzard. We are staying here, where it's safe."

"Safe and BORING!"

"Stop arguing Tom, it's decided," said Gwen. Tom stomped into his cave in fury, and Emily could hear him swiping the walls with his tail on the way in. She sympathised with him, but decided not to say so. Instead she made her parents promise to wake her before the bird departed, and trudged into her room. For a few lovely minutes, she had thought they might be able to join the others, and now their cave had shrunk again!

Gwen woke Emily in the morning, as she had promised.

"The birds are just about to leave," she whispered. "Don't wake Lily. I think we'll leave Tom to sleep in as well – he was so angry last night and I'd rather he didn't see them set off. He might start arguing again!"

Emily tiptoed to the cave entrance, where the buzzard was talking to her father. "Aye, Ah'll tell Sukki tae tell them ye're fine, like," he was saying. " Micht be a bit slower gaein' hame, mind – the wind's turnin' roond. Just oor luck, eh? Hope it doesn'ae blaw intae yer cave." His mate dropped a present of a dead rabbit as he spread his wings and took off. The big birds wheeled together round Ben's head before heading south. They watched as they disappeared into the distance down the glen.

"I hope the message gets through," said Gwen doubtfully.

Duncan had flown up too, and had been watching the buzzards disappear from the top of Ben's head. "He was right, the wind's changing, but there's no sign of a thaw. I think it's about to snow again," he said, coming back. "What shall we do with this rabbit?"

"Leave it out in the snow," his wife advised. "We can't cook it until we can get a decent fire going. It'll keep. I'm not hungry enough for raw rabbit yet. There's Lily awake."

"We won't get snow blowing into the cave will we?" Emily asked, rather worried by the buzzard's remark. So far the north wind had kept their entrance clear.

"The gorse bush will keep us sheltered," her father reassured her, patting snow over the rabbit to keep it fresh and hidden.

"I'm going up to Ben for a look around before it starts to snow again," Emily said, setting off. It felt odd to be standing on Ben's smooth head while all the land was covered in snow. She imagined she could feel a slight warmth coming through her talons, and see faint puffs of his breath in the cold air. If only he was awake; there was no better storyteller!

She gazed all round, but nothing was moving in any direction, not even a crow. It was as if she and her family were the only creatures left alive in this whole white wilderness. She felt close to tears and squeezed her eyes shut.

A touch of snowflakes on her nose made her open them. It was starting to snow again, and this time the flakes were swirling wildly in the wind. As she flew back into the shelter of the cave for breakfast, she hoped her father was right about the gorse bush!

Chapter 6

The Snow Trap

For a while it seemed as though Duncan was right. The veering wind blew all the loose snow into new drifts, exposing the tummy-run in the process, but the gorse bush did seem to be keeping the cave reasonably dry. Each morning there was a little powdery snow in the entrance, but it was easily swept outside before it could melt and cause a bigger problem. Emily and Tom extended their run, and enjoyed some exhilarating slides down the hill, until the bitter wind drove them back inside.

It felt as though the world had been white forever. It was the coldest winter the youngsters had ever known, and even their parents said it was years since they'd had so much snow. (Though of course, there had been MUCH worse winters when they were young!) Every day seemed the same.

Then late one afternoon, five days after the buzzards had left, they all felt a change in the weather. But instead of the thaw they were hoping for, snow clouds massed in the gathering dusk, and the wind veered again, this time coming from the south. As she went to bed, Emily realised that Duncan was looking more than usually worried, and had a restless night, tossing and turning in her heather.

When she got up, earlier than usual, nobody else was awake. Creeping quietly into the main cave, she had a shock. The inside of the cave was pitch black. She sent up a tiny huff of flame, wondering if it was the middle of the night after all, and then she saw the reason. A huge snowdrift had built up in the night, covering their gorse bush and completely blocking the entrance. A good deal had spilled onto the floor of the cave and was melting into pools at the fireplace. The little fire was out, but the rock floor was still warm.

Her shout of "DAD!!" brought the rest of the family tumbling out of their rooms, scattering heather. They all stood surveying the blocked doorway in consternation.

"We can't get out!" Tom whispered, sounding unusually subdued.

"That south wind!" Duncan muttered. "I should have thought!"

"Nothing you could have done," said his wife. "Don't worry, Tom, I'm sure we can huff our way out. I wonder if the snow has stopped. This might just be a new drift of the old snow."

"I bet it's still snowing," said Emily miserably. "What are we going to do? The cave feels so cold!" She shivered.

"We daren't risk a fire. It might cause a flood!" said Duncan. "Then we'd be in an even worse mess."

Lily sensed that everyone was worried and started to wail.

"I said we should have gone with those birds!" Tom muttered.

"Breakfast!" said Gwen hurriedly before an argument could start. "I've got just enough of Ellen's wasp waffles left and we can have them with honey. Not too much, though – I want it to last. Light a couple of huff-torches, Duncan." Lily cheered up at the prospect of honey, and the others felt more hopeful when they were full.

Duncan took his final waffle and his huff-hotted tea and wandered over to check the wall of snow. "This looks the thinnest place," he said through a mouthful, prodding the snow. "Shouldn't be a problem getting out."

In fact it was a difficult job, and took most of the morning. The top of the wall of snow was too high for them to reach, so they started to tunnel their way out, scraping the snow away with talons. They had made quite a deep cave, with still no sign of daylight, when the roof fell in, burying Tom completely. They heard his muffled yell before Gwen rushed over, and she and Duncan scrabbled frantically until the spike of his tail appeared. With a little more digging they were able to haul him out backwards, covered in snow and spluttering.

"Shake off as much snow as you can," Duncan advised.

"Jump around to warm up," Gwen added. "We can't light a fire 'til we can let the smoke out."

Tom danced around energetically, and Lily joined in, giggling. The others stared dejectedly at the wall of snow. "No nearer getting out!" said Duncan.

Emily moved further back, avoiding Lily, and looked up. "We might be," she said. "I think I can see a wee bit of daylight at the top."

"Well spotted," said her dad, looking at the place where she was pointing, and he took off and hovered, nearly bumping his head on the roof. "I think I'll risk a huff and see what happens. Stand back!"

His burst of flame lit up the cave, and caused a small avalanche of snow. Everyone moved further back, and Tom stopped jumping to watch. Another sweep of flame from side to side, and the hole was just big enough for a small dragon to squeeze through. Duncan dropped to the floor.

"Right, Tom," he said, when he had got his breath back, "see if you can get through there. But be careful

– we don't want another fall." The wind could be heard now, whistling through the hole he had melted. A few flakes of snow drifted in.

Tom beamed happily. "Out the way, everyone!" he said as he crouched and sprang up to the roof. With a frantic scrabble, which dislodged more snow, he forced his way through the hole, and they heard a muffled yell and a noise of sliding. "TOM! Are you all right?" shouted Gwen. There was silence, then Tom's voice came through, sounding muffled. "Yes, I'm OK. There's a huge drift here – I slid right down it. Can't see the gorse bush at all. Can't see much, actually – there's too much snow blowing about."

"Can I go out, Dad?" asked Emily eagerly.

"Well done, Tom!" Duncan called. "Could Emily get through?"

"Probably."

"Go and try, Emily. Then I'll melt a bit more and come through myself."

"Huff your way out if you get stuck." Her mother sounded anxious.

Emily flew up to the hole, gripped the edge with her talons, folded her wings tight and forced her way in. It was a very tight fit, but soon her head was out and she was able to look down the long slope of snow in front of her. Tom looked up. "Slide down," he yelled. She squeezed out and slid down head first, landing in a heap at the bottom. "Well done," said Tom. "She's out!" he yelled to the others in the cave.

Emily got her breath back and looked around. She couldn't see very far; as Tom had said the snow was swirling all round them and it was difficult to tell whether it was new snow or loose drifts blowing in the wind. The place looked entirely different, with no sign of the gorse bush and a huge drift filling the flat space between Ben's boots where they usually had their cooking fire. His boots had disappeared, and a smooth snow slope stretched right up to the ledge of his knees. She started to tremble with fear at the strangeness of it, and hoped that Tom would just think she was shivering with cold.

Duncan landed beside them, scattering snow. Even he looked daunted by the huge snowdrift. "We won't shift that in a hurry," he muttered, and flew up to Ben's head to survey the rest of the scene. Emily and Tom joined him, but they could see very little through the whirling snow. They huddled together in silence, Tom not even perching on Ben's ear, as he usually did. "What are we going to do?" Emily asked in a shaking voice.

"I don't know," Duncan admitted, and Emily was pleased that Tom didn't mention the decision not to fly south with the buzzards. Things were far too serious to start an argument! "We'll just have to make that hole bigger and stay put until the weather changes. We do have plenty of food left...." His voice trailed off as he remembered that lighting a fire would be difficult. "Let's get back down."

As they flew down to the bottom of the drift, Emily wondered if Ben was safe under his snowy blanket, but she decided not to mention it. They had enough to worry about. Duncan sent the children back though the hole, telling them to look after Lily while Mum came out. It wasn't much warmer inside, but they danced round in a ring, playing a singing game to amuse Lily while they warmed up.

They could hear their parents talking outside, but their voices were muffled and presently they squeezed back in.

"Nothing we can do while this wind keeps up," said Duncan, "but I think the weather's improving. It *has* stopped – that's just blowing snow outside. And there's a tiny bit of blue sky. Give it an hour or so, and we'll go out again."

It was hard to wait, but Emily took Tom and Lily into her room and read to them while Gwen and Duncan tidied up the blown snow and the water on the cave floor. They also enlarged the hole, enough to light a small fire so that most of the smoke could escape, and had another look at the weather outside. Finally Duncan reported that it was brighter and calmer, and they could all go outside, even Lily. One by one they squeezed through the hole and slid down the drift.

There was still some blowing snow, but much less, and the sky had cleared for the first time in many days. It was still bitterly cold, but the brightness made them all feel better. It still looked impossible to see how they could dig through the drift. The trees down the glen were half buried in snow, the stream was hardly visible, and the only distinct feature to break up the whiteness was the head and shoulders of Ben McIlwhinnie, still free of snow. Tiny white puffs reassured them that he was still breathing.

"Of course he is!" Gwen said when Emily looked relieved. "He's lived up here for centuries! He must have known lots of winters just as bad as this."

"I still think we could go and find the others, now it's stopped snowing," said Tom.

"It could start again any time. And how could we find them? Not worth the risk."

"I know things are uncomfortable, but it won't last forever," Gwen said, trying to sound more confident than she felt.

"Let's at least try a Huff in the gloaming," said Emily. "Someone might see it."

"Who?" Tom sounded scornful.

"We can try if you like," said Duncan, but Emily could tell that he was only saying that to make her feel better. He didn't believe anyone would see it.

"Go for a fly to stretch your wings. I'll stay with Lily," Duncan suggested.

The other three took off down the glen. It was quite difficult to see where the loch was in the deep snow. The whole landscape looked quite different. The stream was still visible from above, but now sunk deep in snow banks. Then they flew over to check on the tree house, and found it almost invisible inside its snow blanket. The leafless trees looked stark and black against the snow, but a few of the fir trees had blown down in the gales, and several had branches torn off with the weight of snow. They could see the tracks of deer and wondered how they were finding enough to eat. At the edge of the wood they saw a dead stag, half covered, and the sight made the young dragons realise how dangerous winter could be. The crows had gathered, and Gwen swooped and swiped a couple with her tail before they turned for home.

They were all feeling worried. How long was this weather going to last?

Inside the cave, the huff-torches were glowing, hot drinks were waiting and they began to feel better. Emily reminded Duncan about the Gloaming Huff, and he agreed to fly up before the light faded.

"I can't think anyone will be out looking for this," he said, between Huffs. "But I suppose it's a while since we've seen a sunset!" It was certainly a spectacular one, Emily thought, with the pink and red sky lighting up the snow. The moon was rising. She gazed all round, hopefully, but there was no sign of an answering Huff.

"Well, we tried!" said Duncan, watching his column of smoke waver and fade in the darkening sky. "Let's risk a fire tonight now the smoke-hole is bigger. Cheer up! It might start thawing tomorrow."

"I think it's even colder," said Emily despondently. Duncan sighed as he followed her down. He had a feeling she was right!

Chapter 7

In the Middle of the Night

Duncan had no idea what woke him in the middle of the night. Was it Lily? No, she was curled up, fast asleep. Perhaps the sound of a hunting owl had penetrated into the cave? He lay listening, then crept out of the heather and made his way into the dark outer cave. There was the faintest moonlight glow from the opening high in the snow wall, but all was silent. He was just about to go back to bed when he heard it again; a slithering, scraping noise from the snowdrift outside. Something was trying to get in!

As quietly as he could, he flew up to the hole, thrust his head through and sent a jet of flame into the night. There was a muffled yell, a slither and then into the silence came a voice. "Suffering Huffs! You nearly burnt my ears off!!"

Duncan peered down in amazement. "*Des??*" He could just make out the shape of a dragon half buried in the snowdrift.

"Of course it's me! Who did you think it was?" With a mighty heave Des shook the snow off his wings and gazed up at Duncan, whose head was just visible through the hole. "Are you stuck in there?"

"No, we can just about get in and out!" Duncan squeezed through and landed beside Des. They clapped wings. "What are you doing here? I thought you were safe in the castle with the others. Is something wrong?"

"Not with them! They're all fine. It's you lot I was worried about. Sukki got a pal of hers to fly up to check, but we never heard back from him. Then when the wind veered south, I thought you might be in trouble up here, so when the snow stopped and the wind dropped a bit, I decided to come and see. Looks as though I was just in time. You'll not be able to shift this drift in a hurry. Must be pretty cold in there. Are the kids OK?"

"Yes. Just bored and grumpy! We were managing OK until the wind changed last night and this built up. We had to dig ourselves out. Come inside and I'll fix you a hot drink and a bed for the rest of the night. Be quiet, though. We'll give them a shock in the morning!" He scrambled up the drift and squeezed into the cave and Des followed, landing on the floor with such a bang that they held their breath, waiting for Lily to wail and wake the rest of the family; but there was silence.

"There's spare heather in the Bone Cave," said Duncan, huffing a mug of nettle beer. "See you in the morning, and you can tell us everything over breakfast. It's great to see you, mate! Thanks!" he added. Des grinned cheerfully and disappeared with his beer, leaving a trail of melted snow across the cave floor. Duncan smiled to himself, feeling suddenly a lot happier. He was looking forward to seeing Emily's face in the morning!

Everybody woke late again, the children hoping that the wall of snow might have disappeared by magic overnight, and slumping grumpily when they found it was still there. Gwen had gone out to check on the weather, and Duncan was dishing out food as quietly as he could, being careful not to glance too obviously in the direction of the Bone Cave

"That drift might be there for weeks!" Tom complained to Emily over a cold breakfast. "We can't just stay cooped up here. I'm going mad!"

"Me too," Emily agreed. "Go away, Lily!" she added crossly, and didn't even relent when her sister gave her the big-eyed pleading look which usually worked so well. Lily stomped off in a huff and swung her tail at the pile of pebbles she'd built for Emily to admire. They fell with a loud clatter.

There was a groan from inside the Bone Cave.

"AAAH!! I'd forgotten what a noisy lot you are first thing in the morning."

Tom and Emily sprang up. "What...?" "Who's that....?" "DES??" They rushed to the entrance, crammed themselves through, and hurled themselves on Des. He had been trying to get up, but fell back under the onslaught.

"Get off!! How can I get up with you two sitting on me?"

"When did you get here?"

"*How* did you get here?"

Des waggled his wings at Tom.

"Did you see our Huff?"

"Are the others here too?"

Des shook his head, pushed them away and got to his feet.

"Right, it's good to see you too! Let me get out, give me some breakfast, and then I'll tell you whatever you want to know." They each took a wing and towed him into the main cave, where Duncan was laughing, and Gwen was peering through from outside, watching them all. Lily gave Des her most appealing smile, and smirked triumphantly at Emily as he picked her up and swung her above his head. "You've grown!" he said.

"Never mind Lily!" said Tom. "Tell us why you're here."

"And how the others are," added Emily. "Oh, Des, it's SO lovely to see you!" For the first time in days she looked happy, and her parents smiled at each other in relief.

Emily and Tom managed a second breakfast to keep Des company and then everyone gathered round, eager to hear his news.

"Well, the others are all missing you, but everyone's fine," he started. "It's been snowing there too, so they've been stuck in, but the old place is huge compared to this cave, so they're not so cooped up. They've been managing quite a lot of exercise, even when they were stuck inside. Angie's behaving herself, sort of. There've been a few rows. George was pretty exhausted by the time we got there, and we were a bit worried, but he's all right now, and tries to keep the peace between Ange and Ellen, which can be tricky. There's lots of food, so nobody goes hungry."

"Haven't you seen any Humans?" Dad asked, voicing his chief worry

"Not close to the castle. I've seen a few when I've gone out foraging, but I've managed not to get

71

spotted. A couple of kestrels, pals of Sukki, live near and they've agreed to give us warning if any Humans come snooping. I sent them to Sukki with the message for you. Did it arrive?"

"Yes, two buzzards turned up several days ago, and took a message back. Didn't you get it?"

"No. Don't know why not. But when nothing came, I decided to come up myself. Wasn't a bad journey, with the wind behind me. I did it in a day."

"You flew in daylight!"

"Yep!"

"Honestly, Des...."

"Listen Duncan, this snow's changed everything! The whole country's covered. Hardly anything's moving at all. There are Humans out round their villages and places, and the birds say there are plenty of them sliding around on the high mountains, but if you choose your route, it's OK. Quite safe. Obviously it'll take longer with all of us, but there's no danger from Humans at the moment, trust me."

"ALL of us?" Gwen repeated, sounding dazed.

"YESS!!" Tom shouted, but was ignored.

"Don't talk rubbish, Des. It's great to see you, and we'll be glad of some help up here, but we can't leave this place and come south with you. The children would never manage it. And what about Lily?"

"Ellen sent Georgie's sling, so Lily will be fine. We can give Emily and Tom lifts between us if they need them, but I bet they won't. You don't realise what good flyers they've become this year. We can fly at night if you'd feel happier. I know the way. Where's the problem?"

"We can't expect Angie to take us all in!" Gwen sounded tempted, Emily thought.

"She wants you to come. She knows you'll all help with foraging and cooking and things. And if it keeps the kids happy, the place will be a lot more peaceful, believe me! There's lots of food, like I said. Come on, Duncan! This cave will still be here when the winter's over and you come back. You know you'll all be trapped if this snow carries on and that drift keeps piling up. As soon as the wind changed I knew you'd be in trouble, and I was right!"

There was a long silence, and Emily held her breath. Tom opened his mouth, but she gave him a warning nudge with her tail. Better to leave it to Des! She had missed Alice so much, and now it looked as though she might see her very soon. And she loved the idea of a castle! She shut her eyes and willed her father to agree.

Finally he broke the expectant silence. "What do you think, Gwen?" All eyes turned to their mother.

"If you're *quite* sure there's room and food enough for all of us, I think we should go," she said slowly. "As long as we can take the children safely. We can't cook proper meals or keep warm with no decent fire, and we'll all start to suffer if this snow goes on much longer. There's no sign of a thaw further south, I suppose?" She looked at Des, who shook his head. "Then I vote we go."

It was obvious that Duncan still had grave doubts, but equally obvious that the children were very keen to go. He blew a long thoughtful huff up to the roof of the cave and then looked round all the eager faces.

"All right, we'll go. And just hope this cave stays safe and empty until we get back."

"Ben will look after it!" Emily beamed.

"Ben is asleep, dimwit!" said Tom. "When can we start, Des?"

"How's the weather, Gwen?"

"Not blowing as hard, and the sky's clear at the moment."

"Then as soon as we can. No need to take anything, apart from ourselves and food for the journey."

"There're things to pack away safely in here. And we can't arrive empty-clawed. Take these three out for an hour while we get ready," Gwen suggested, heading for the shelves.

Des tucked Lily under one arm, and followed Tom and Emily through the hole. "Is the loch frozen? How are the otters managing?"

"They've gone," Emily told him as they took wing.

"Really? You HAVE been abandoned!" Des exclaimed. "Where've they gone?"

"To the big river, they said."

"We've got a great new game going on the loch," said Tom eagerly. "It's called Tail-Stane. I'll show you. Is there a frozen loch near the castle? We could have a fantastic game with all of us. I can't wait to show Ollie."

But when they reached the loch and landed he was disappointed. Their spare pebble pile had vanished under the blanket of snow, and so had most of the ice. Only a small area was swept clear enough for a decent slide, and they all ended up half-buried in the drift at the far end. Lily clung onto Des's spikes, laughing even when she flew off at the sudden stop and landed nose-first in the drift. They fished her out, still giggling, and slid back.

"I hope you won't be too disappointed with Angie's place," Des warned, as they flew back to the cave. "I didn't want to say too much in front of Duncan, but we do have to watch out for Humans all the time. There is a wee loch not far away, but when I flew past on my way here, there were lots of Humans sliding all over it, and some of those machines of theirs nearby. I had to dodge through the trees to keep out of sight. I suspect Tail-Stane will be out – sorry Tom!"

Tom said nothing, but a stubborn expression came over his face. Emily hoped he would keep quiet about it until they were safely on their way. He did, to her relief. He really was a lot more sensible these days!

Chapter 8

Disaster Strikes

The sun was still quite high when they set out, and as they had done on earlier daylight expeditions, they flew high and close together. Gwen carried a wriggling Lily in her sling, but fortunately she was tired after playing in the snow and soon fell asleep. Emily realised that they were following the same track that she and the others had taken in the hunt for Ollie, but this time they gave the building site a wide berth in case any Humans were around. There was no sound of loud machines, and Des reported that the site seemed to be deserted.

"One good thing about snow – it keeps Humans away," he remarked, seeing their big machines in the distance, motionless in the snow. "Anyone need a rest?"

"Let's keep going while the light lasts," said Gwen. "Say if you need a lift, kids."

"I'm fine," said Emily, and Tom agreed. The wind had dropped a little, though it was still against them, and the sun was beginning to sink. There was no break in the snow cover as far as they could see into the distance.

"We'll get right out of the glen and then have a break," Des decided. "There's some good thick woodland ahead and that'll give us some cover and a bit of shelter. After that we're nearer to Human settlements, so we'd be better flying in the dark."

They flew on and on as the sun sank into a bank of cloud on the horizon and the air got colder. Des gave Tom a lift, and Gwen passed Lily over to Duncan, as she had woken and popped her head out of the sling to watch where they were going. Emily began to feel weary, but as the sky darkened, Des pointed ahead. "That's the start of the wood," he called. "Let's get into the shelter there and take a break. We'll feel better if we have something to eat."

They flew lower as they reached the trees, and Des led them into the wood. Even in the shelter it was bitterly cold, so, despite Duncan's misgivings, they lit a small fire and huddled round it while Gwen passed food around. It started to snow, large flakes filtering through the branches overhead. "Probably most of that's blowing off the branches," Des said reassuringly when Gwen started to look worried. "But we'd better get going again, I think." He jumped the fire out and led the way out of the trees.

The wind hit them as they emerged. Outside the wood, the lying snow had started to blow in the wind, so that it looked as though there was thick mist near the ground. As they took off, the ground below blurred, so they could see no features, and only the trees showed black against the white blanket. Night was coming on, but there would be no chance of moon or stars to guide them tonight. Thick cloud covered the sky and the snow swirled thicker around them. They flew as close together as they could, following Des, but the wind slowed them and Duncan soon realised that they could not go on. He flew up beside Des.

"This is no good. Wind's too strong. Can't see. Anywhere safe to shelter 'til it eases off?"

"We've passed the belt of trees. Wide valley now. No shelter. More trees ahead. We'll head for them. Don't worry. Know where we are."

Duncan dropped back beside Tom.

"Can you keep going? We'll stop soon. Find shelter. OK?"

The children nodded, too frightened and exhausted to speak. Just trying to fly in a straight line was enough of an effort!

"Lower!" yelled Des, veering downwards. "Need to see the ground!"

He led them downwards. Suddenly, through the howling of the wind, Emily thought she heard a strange high singing noise. She was about to ask when there was a yell from Des. He sounded terrified.

"Up, UP! Singing Strings! UP!!!"

Emily and Tom had no idea what he meant, but the panic in his voice was enough. There was a flurry of wings and tails as they all tried to change direction and avoid the noise, which had suddenly grown louder and more menacing. Duncan and Tom collided in mid-air, and Tom was knocked off course.

He spiralled downwards, flailing his wings to regain his balance, buffeted helplessly by the wind. In seconds he was out of sight. His father dived to follow him. Emily's scream stopped Des and Gwen from climbing higher. They hovered in the air, blinded by snow and buffeted by the wind. The singing seemed to grow louder but above it there was a crash, a yell and a scream of "DAD!"

"Oh NO!" said Des. Gwen and Emily were too horrified to say anything. Des took charge. "Follow me very close. We're heading straight for the ground. Don't lose sight of each other. Go!"

They headed blindly down. The singing grew fainter. As he dropped, Des shouted for Tom, and soon they heard a faint cry and Tom appeared through the snow. "Dad fell!" he gasped. He was shaking and scarcely able to fly. "Nearly down" Des shouted, and suddenly they all pitched headlong into deep snow and lay, panting and exhausted.

Des recovered almost immediately, and shook Tom. "Did he hit the Strings?" he demanded urgently.

"N-no, there was a huge cage-thing in the sky. He hit that. He was trying to save me."

"Right. I'll find him. You stay here. Dig yourselves in and stay together." Gwen nodded as Des disappeared into the storm.

Des set off. He knew what Duncan had hit – one of the huge metal towers built by Humans to carry the Singing Strings across the countryside. Des had no idea what they were, but he knew they were very dangerous, especially the Strings which were avoided by birds as well as dragons. He stopped and listened. He could still hear the singing, even above the wind. He knew the note would change as it neared the tower. He plodded on in the white wilderness, not daring to fly, seeing nothing but listening hard. He was blaming himself, bitterly. How could he have forgotten those Strings across the valley? Now Duncan might be dead, if he had hit the Strings before the tower.

The note changed. He stopped, straining ears and eyes.

Nothing.

"DUNCAN!" he yelled into the whiteness.

Nothing.

He followed the singing, stopping at intervals to shout. There was no answering call.

In another few steps he glimpsed a new shape in front of him and stopped; one foot of the metal tower, half buried in the snow. The structure loomed above him, the top lost in the swirling flakes. The singing had almost died away. He made his way towards it treading carefully. When he reached it he shouted again, and his heart sank when there was still no reply. Where was Duncan? He must be near. Cautiously, trying to keep the foot of the tower in sight, he moved to his left, and soon saw the second foot. Still no Duncan. He turned right, remembering the square shape of the towers, and then he spotted a dark shape lying motionless in the snow in front of him.

Gwen took charge as Des disappeared. She was terrified, but knew that she must keep the children calm.

Lily had woken and was wailing, so she handed her to Tom, who was still shaking. "Keep her wrapped in the sling and cuddle her close," she ordered. "Emily, help me to dig!" They began scrabbling frantically into the snow bank with their talons. Under the recent fall it was hard packed and needed Huff to melt a small round cave. Into this the four of them huddled, gazing out into the whiteness. Out of the wind it was slightly warmer and they could talk without shouting.

"Will Dad be OK?" Emily asked in a trembling voice.

"I don't know. Des will find him."

"It was all my fault!" Tom sounded tearful.

"No it wasn't!" said his mother firmly.

"How long d'you think they'll be?"

"I don't know," Gwen wished that she had some food to distract them, but Duncan had been carrying the bag. "We just have to wait. We're safe in here."

"Can you do another big Huff, Mum? They might see it."

"Good idea!" Anything was better than waiting in the dark and the cold, Gwen thought. A Huff would warm them, and there was no chance of it being spotted! She sent a burst of flame into the sky. Even the brief light cheered them a little and gave them hope, but when it died the night seemed even darker. There was no sound above the wind except the faint singing of the Strings in the distance. She shuddered. She knew, from old Dragon lore, that they were deadly. They should never have come! She blamed herself bitterly.

"Mum..."

"Yes?"

"Can we try shouting?"

Des reached the sprawled shape, terrified. Already the snow was starting to cover Duncan's body. There was blood on the snow by his head, and one wing was bent at an odd angle. He reached out a cautious claw. "Duncan!" he whispered. "Please..."

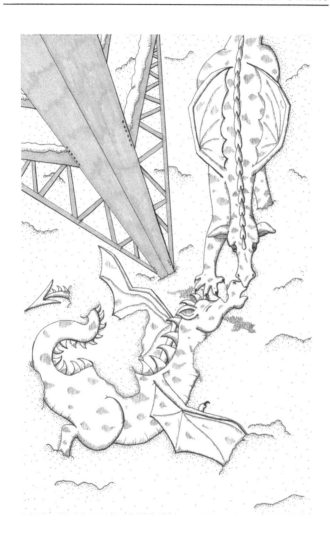

To his enormous relief, the dark blue body stirred. "Des..?"

"Yes, it's me. And the others are all right, not far away."

"Tom...?"

"He got a fright, but he's OK."

"He was going to hit the Strings..."

"Then you saved his life. Can you walk?"

Duncan clambered painfully to his feet. "Think so. Must've hit my head."

"Your wing doesn't look too good. But never mind that now. Come on, we'll walk back to the others. It's not far."

Grabbing the fallen food bag, and supporting the staggering Duncan, Des set off, retracing his footprints. They were fast filling up with snow, and he hoped they would lead him back to the others. When they were a bit nearer he could shout. They battled on. It seemed further now. Had he lost them?

Suddenly a flare lit up the night in front of them. "Gwen's sent up a Huff!" he said in relief. "Nearly there. Just another few steps..."

The anxious watchers sent up three Huffs of relief as they saw TWO shadowy figures staggering towards them through the snow.

Chapter 9

Waiting for Help

"What are you doing, Des?"

The quiet voice came from behind him, and Des jumped guiltily. Turning round, he saw Gwen looking at him with the sort of expression she usually reserved for her children on a bad day. It was the middle of the night, but the sky had cleared and the moon was high, lighting up the wide expanse of snow. Stars glittered overhead.

"Er..."

Gwen pushed him aside and read the letters he had been scraping in the snow.

"GON TO GET HELP BAK SOON ST... You're *leaving!*"

"Ssshh! Don't wake the others. Come over here." He led her away from the snow cave in which the children and an exhausted Duncan were sleeping in an untidy heap and whispered urgently. "Gwen, I HAVE to get help! Duncan will be OK, but his wing's broken. He can't fly. You and I couldn't possibly carry him between us and we can't *walk* to the castle. We can't stay here either. We need help!"

"You mean the others?"

"I promise I won't be long!" Des avoided the question. "Listen, I flew to the river a few minutes ago, and there's a tumble of rocks beside it – big ones. You could walk there easily, and it would be a better shelter and hiding place until I come back. It's not far. You'll see them when it's light. Now that I've told you, we can forget the message. I'm going. Fast as I can fly. See you soon. Look after the others."

Gwen gave him a long steady look, but he could see tears in her eyes. "Be careful," she said.

Des tried a grin. "Me???"

"Yes, I mean it!" She gave him a quick hug and stood back as he spread his wings and took off. From above, he saw her turn and crawl back into the little cave. Heaving a sigh of relief he changed direction in mid air and headed north.

Back inside the snow shelter, Gwen found it very difficult to get back to sleep. She was cold and uncomfortable, and despite Des's reassurance, very worried indeed. She knew he was right; they would not get to the castle, or even back to their old cave, without help. But they couldn't stay here either. It was far too close to Humans. She could see the great metal tower in the moonlight, and shuddered. They could all have hit the Singing Strings. How *could* she have decided to come south to their friends? She was the one who finally persuaded Duncan. It was all her fault! She knew it was possible to mend a broken wing, but how long would it be before Duncan could fly again?

At least the children seemed warm in their cosy huddle, she thought, but Duncan was stirring and moaning in his sleep. And it was so cold! She dozed fitfully.

The rising sun shone directly into their snow shelter and all the dragons woke early, stiff and sore after the long flight and their cramped night. Gwen was awake before the others, and risked a quick flight to check their surroundings. When the others emerged, Lily bouncing but the others groaning, she handed round a little of the food they had left, and explained what had happened in the night before they could bombard her with questions. Emily had spotted Des's message at once.

"Where's he gone?"

"For help. I'll tell you all I know. Don't interrupt, Tom." She explained Des's plan, reassured them he would be back soon, that the others would be sure to know what to do, and hurried on before they could argue. "I've flown up to check, and there are no Humans around. But we need a better shelter, so we're going to walk a little way to the rocks by the river and hide there 'til Des gets back."

"He won't know where we are," Tom interrupted. "We need to stay here."

"He knows where we'll be. He found the place. How's your head, Duncan? Can you walk? It's not far."

"I'll manage. We should go at once, in case any Humans come up the valley when it's properly light."

"Can we have some more to eat first?" asked Tom.

"When we get there," his mother said firmly, aware that there was very little left, but not wanting to admit it just yet. She pointed to the tumble of rocks in the distance. "It's there, by the river. You kids can fly if you like, but don't get too far ahead, and keep low. We'll *walk* under those Singing Strings!" she added firmly, picking up Lily and the food bag. "Come on!"

Emily and Tom were glad to stretch their wings. They flew low over the blanket of snow with its hummocks and drifts until they were close to the sinister Human tower and could hear the singing of the overhead wires. Then they circled back to where their parents were toiling slowly through the snow. They showed up very clearly, blue against the white. Emily took the food bag, but didn't say anything about how light it seemed. Eventually they reached the line of the Singing Strings and hurried under it as fast as they could.

"Nearly there," said Emily encouragingly. Her father looked exhausted already, and it was obvious that his broken wing, which stuck out at an odd angle, was hurting badly. The rock pile still seemed quite a long way away, despite what she had said.

"You two fly on now we're past that awful place," said Gwen. "Try to find us a good place to hide and then we can have something to eat."

Tom and Emily took to their wings, and soon reached the rocks. Des was right, they provided quite good shelter – not as good as a cave, but it was possible to squeeze between some big ones and find a place that was reasonably free of snow. It had obviously blown right over the top in the blizzard. Tom left Emily sweeping the ground clear with her tail and flew back to their parents. Eventually they arrived and sank down, glad to be out of the wind. Gwen shared out what was left of the food, and they all made their way to the bank of the river for a drink. Even icy water was welcome.

"I wonder if this is the big river the otters have gone to," said Tom.

"No idea," said Duncan. "And the otters would be no help to us in this mess." He sank down between the rocks and closed his eyes. The other three looked at him, worried.

"How long did Des say he would be?" Emily whispered.

"He didn't know. But I know he'll be as quick as he can."

"I hope he brings some food! I'm still hungry," said Tom.

"There might be snails in the cracks of these rocks. Why don't you look?" Gwen suggested, hoping to keep him busy. "Emily, can you find a good look-out place on top of these rocks and keep a watch."

"For Des?"

"Yes, and for danger!" said her mother, following Duncan into the sheltered spot with Lily. "Not that there'll be any," she added, seeing Emily's face, "but it's best to be sure." Emily nodded, and climbed carefully up the nearest rock. The top was in the sun, so she lay down and spread her wings to feel a bit of welcome heat. Then she looked all round. There were no Humans in sight, and only the towers and the Singing Strings gave any sign that they had ever been in this valley. But that was enough!

Then in the distance, in the foothills across the river, she saw a brown moving blur against the snow. She gazed for a few minutes, lying flat, and then realised it was a sizeable herd of the large Red Deer that she remembered from their old glen. They were coming to the river. She hoped they wouldn't wade across. As she watched they drank, then fanned out on the opposite bank, scraping away at the snow with their hooves to get at the grass beneath. A heron flapped slowly down the river and out of sight. Emily thought of the otters again, and wished they would suddenly appear. Preferably with some spare fish! She was hungry again, and tried not to think about food.

Presently there was a scrambling behind her and Tom appeared. "I found some!" he said, handing her a large snail. We've had one each." Emily crunched happily, but it didn't really take her hunger away. She pointed beyond the river.

"I think those might be rowan trees over there. See? Why don't you fly over and see if there are any berries left?"

Tom agreed and flew across the river. The deer lifted their heads and watched as he flew over, and one large stag bellowed a warning. She saw him land in the largest tree, which swayed beneath him and heard a yell. She hoped it was a yell of triumph, and got ready to fly in case it wasn't, but before she could launch herself she saw him turn to come back. "I found a few!" he shouted as he got near. "A bit wrinkly, but better than nothing. But best of all I think I saw a grouse half buried in the snow. I'm going to tell Mum!" He dropped a small bunch of berries on her rock and disappeared. Emily munched them and suddenly remembered she was supposed to be keeping a lookout. She gazed round hastily, but there was nothing in sight that worried her. The sun was sinking and disappearing behind a bank of cloud. She hoped it wasn't going to snow again. How would Des find them in a blizzard? She shivered. The short winter day would end soon, and Des hadn't come back.

She saw her mother fly off across the river and start back with a large bird in her talons, and heard the crackle of a fire beginning below her rock. Dad must have agreed that it was worth the risk. The thought of hot food made her feel much better; taking a last look round, she scrambled down to join the others.

Duncan had slept through most of the day, and was looking a good deal better, though still in pain from his broken wing. Tom was looking proud of himself – he had built the fire and was allowed to light it, and soon the grouse that he had found was plucked and roasting. There was plenty for them all, and when they were full, they felt much more optimistic.

"It's bound to take a while for Des to fetch help," Gwen said reassuringly. "We're warm and fed and safe, and now we just have to wait. You children should get some sleep."

As she said that, there was an ominous rumble in the distance. Tom, who had been crunching the very last bone, stopped and they all listened. It grew louder. And LOUDER!! Duncan pulled Emily back as she was about to scramble out of shelter to look. "Hide!" he shouted above the din, "that's a Human machine!"

They were just in time to crouch under an over-hanging rock. Gwen jumped the fire out and scrambled to join them as the noise became deafening and a bright beam of light shone down among the rocks. Peering up, Emily could see a huge machine above them, and feel a strong wind from turning blades that blew the snow into blinding swirls. They all put their wings over their ears, trembling. They felt the ground shake as the deer stampeded in fright. It seemed as though the Human machine had been hovering above them for hours when suddenly it tilted and veered away across the river and up into the hills opposite. The noise faded, but it took a long time for it to disappear completely.

Gwen drew a shaky breath. "Were there Humans in that thing? Do you think they saw us?"

"Hope not. I guess they spotted our smoke though. Narrow escape! If Des doesn't come by tomorrow morning we'll have to move. We can't risk Humans coming on foot to check up."

Gwen said nothing. She couldn't see how they could move far, but it was not the time to discuss it. "Bed, kids. Lily can cuddle up between you," she said firmly. "You get some sleep too, Duncan. I'll keep watch." She crept up to Emily's rock, lay flat and gazed into the valley. The deer had gone. She heard her family settle down to sleep. Safe for now, she thought, as the moon rose and lit up the snow. But where had Des disappeared to?

Chapter 10

Ben to the Rescue

Flying back north as fast as he could, helped by the wind, Des got to the cave in record time and there was still plenty of daylight left when he arrived. The drift blocking the cave was even bigger, but he had a more important thing to do before he tried to force his way in.

There was only one person who could get them out of this predicament – and he was asleep. He was also half buried in snow. Des considered his options. Obviously shouting Ben's name would have no effect. He was sleeping too deeply. Back in the summer, gentle huffs up his nostrils had been enough, but Des doubted whether it would work in the middle of winter. However it was worth a try. Gently at first, then harder and harder he huffed, but the only response was a sleepy snort which blew Des off his perch. That was some progress, Des thought, trying not to feel too desperate – but he had no time to waste. He didn't dare resort to a flare!

Right, nose no good; how about ears? He flew up to Tom's favourite perch and leaned down, blowing into Ben's ear. Then he filled his lungs and shouted as loudly as he could, "BEN! BEN!! WAKE UP!!!" He waited, hoping to see the huge eyes open, but nothing happened. "BEN, THE DRAGONS NEED YOU!!!" There was still no response, so he tried the other ear, huffing the snow off it first, and yelling at the top of his lungs. He had stopped to get his breath back, and was beginning to despair when a faint shudder ran through the huge body. He shouted into the ear again, "HELP, BEN, HELP!!" and finally in desperation "EMILY NEEDS YOU! EMILY!!!"

The huge eyes opened and blinked a few times, slowly. Then Ben took a deep breath, smoky as a dragon's in the cold air. "Emily?" said his deep voice.

Des hovered in front of him. "No it's me, Des! Sorry to wake you but I need help. The dragons are trouble, Emily and Tom are in danger... please help, you're the only person who can save them..." Des was falling over his words in his haste to make Ben understand.

"Hmmm. I might have known it would be you, young Desmond! But this sounds serious. In danger you say? How can I help? Are they here? Is it Humans?"

Des went back to his perch, as Ben now seemed fully awake. He took a deep breath and tried to keep the shake out of his voice. "They're away south of here. They had to move out of the cave because of the snow. Duncan has a broken wing. Ben – could you manage to stand up and walk south to carry him to safety? You're the only one who can help. I'll show you the way. Please!" He crossed his fingers, toes and tail and waited.

Ben's head moved from side to side and up and down as he took in his surroundings. "Hmmm. I seem to be covered in a good deal of snow. But I will attempt to rise to my feet. You had better fly clear. I may cause a small avalanche. Hands first, I think."

As Des watched in astonishment and delight, he wriggled his huge fingers clear of the snow and the earth under it, brushed the drift off his knees, shook his shoulders and slowly, very slowly, rose to his full enormous height. The snowdrift covering the cave entrance cascaded down the hill and the gorse bush reappeared. Ben's boots were still buried, the snow reaching half-way to his knees.

"Will you be able to walk?" asked Des, awestruck.

"I think so, given a little time. I must try to remember how to do it. It's many, many years since I tried."

"While you work it out, I'll check inside the cave to make sure it's OK," said Des, worried that the earthquake of Ben's movement might have caused a rock fall. To his relief it hadn't; Ben's chair obviously made a solid roof. He hastily found one of his old travelling bags and stuffed in as much food as would fit.

"Can we go?" he said, rushing out again. "It really is urgent! I can tell you the whole story on the way, but the sooner we reach them the better. I promised Gwen I'd be as quick as I could."

"Did she ask you to come for me?"

"No, it was my idea."

Ben chuckled. "You have almost as many ideas as our clever young Emily. Is there a risk they might be seen by Humans where they are?"

"I hope not."

"I would like to remain unseen myself, which might prove difficult. I am not afraid of Humans, of course, but would prefer not to become an object of interest. I suggest we travel mainly in the dark, but the sun is nearly down, so we could begin our journey down this empty glen. Find yourself a secure perch and we'll go."

Des wedged himself around the spindly trunk of a small elder tree which had rooted itself near Ben's right ear, looped his food bag securely round his tail and watched in amazement as the giant lifted one boot clear of the snow and took a mighty stride forward. Slowly at first, as his legs came free of the drift, then faster, he made his way down the glen, taking huge strides. In no time at all they reached the loch, skirted it, and headed south. The sun set behind a cloud bank. Soon they would be safe under cover of darkness. Des started to enjoy himself. He was sure they would reach the others in time and all would be well.

At the site of the old castle, Ben paused briefly. "So many Humans killed in this place," he said softly, as if to himself. "I must not be seen near here, or we risk this glen being invaded again. Desmond, keep a sharp lookout while you tell me how it is that our friends are in such trouble."

Swaying to the regular movement of Ben's enormous strides, and gazing round for possible danger, Des told Ben the whole story; of the departure of Alice and Ollie and their family, the coming of the snow, the blocking of the cave and finally the attempt to escape to the south for the rest of the winter. "And it was all going fine until the blizzard last night," he concluded. "It was my fault! I completely forgot about the Singing Strings in the valley. Tom lost his balance in the blizzard, and when Duncan dived to save him, he hit the Humans' tower, knocked himself out and broke a wing. So I had to leave them all in shelter while I came to you for help."

"Hmmm, I hope they haven't been discovered. Perhaps I should walk a little faster. Hold tight!"

They were making fantastic progress, Des thought, mentally ticking off the landmarks as they passed. He was finding it quite hard to stay awake after the efforts of the previous night, especially when he became aware that Ben was humming to himself. The sonorous rhythm was very soothing, but he MUSTN'T fall asleep. He stayed awake by picturing their triumphant arrival in the valley, and beamed as he imagined how surprised the family would be.

Then a dreadful thought struck him!

"BEN!" he shouted in alarm, and the humming stopped.

"Have we lost our way?" Ben enquired.

"No, and we're not far away now. But I forgot the Singing Strings again! I don't think you can walk underneath without hitting them. Have you seen them before?"

"I have no idea what you are talking about, young Desmond," Ben admitted, continuing with his steady stride. "Remember it is many years since I left my seat in the glen. The world may have changed. But the night is clear and we should see danger before we meet it. Then we can decide what to do. I can see the edge of this wood to my right, so I will skirt round it. No point in killing innocent trees by tramping them down."

Looking back in the moonlight, Des could see the line of enormous footprints Ben was leaving behind him. He wondered what the Humans would make of those if they spotted them, and chuckled. They were even better than the dragon prints that had so intrigued the little Human family on the beach in the summer. He remembered how much Emily had enjoyed seeing the children, and hoped she and the others were safe.

They strode on, getting nearer to the river valley. Des strained his eyes to try and spot the towers and the Singing Strings. He needed to give Ben plenty of warning in case he walked into them. He was distracted by the sight of a large herd of deer on the edge of the hill. A big stag got to its feet and stared at them, but to Des's surprise, the herd didn't rise and flee. It was as though they recognised that they were in no danger from this huge Giant pacing silently and steadily across the snowy land.

There was still a good deal of the night left when Des, straining his eyes, spotted the lines of the Singing Strings in the distance. He warned Ben, who came to a standstill and gazed ahead. "I have never seen anything like that before," he mused. "How strange and unnatural those towers look in this valley. Only Humans could have thought of those. Do you think they are dangerous?"

"I KNOW they are! If you fly into those Strings, there is a flash of light and you die. All birds and dragons know that."

"Let us get a little nearer and see how we can pass in safety. Is it not possible to walk around the end?"

"There is no end. That's the problem. They go on forever, marching over rivers and hills. You can fly over or crawl under, but there's no other way through."

"Hmmm! Humans!" said Ben grimly. "I could smash those towers like twigs, but I fear it would do no good in the end." He came to a stop, close enough to the towers to judge their height. "You are right, young Desmond. I am too tall to pass under these Strings, as you call them. What a strange and haunting song they sing."

Desmond felt like bursting into tears. So near to saving the dragons, and he was being thwarted by Humans again! "What are we going to do?" he said wretchedly. "Emily and the others are very near, on the other side. I don't suppose you can crawl through on your hands and knees, can you?"

"I do not bend easily," said Ben.

"I wanted you to take Duncan and the family to the castle to stay with the others," Des said sadly. "I'm sure Old George would know how to mend Duncan's broken wing, and they would be safe with their friends while it heals. But if we can't get through, we can't! I'll fly over and bring them here. You can carry them back home. They'll be safer back in the cave. I'm sorry, Ben. I've woken you up for nothing."

111

"Not so fast, young Desmond. Let me think."

Desmond waited for what seemed a long time, hardly daring to hope. Finally Ben spoke again. "I WILL NOT ALLOW THE HUMANS TO WIN!" His deep voice boomed through the valley. "Desmond, fly to our friends and warn them. I will put an end to these Singing Strings!"

Des took off from his perch and headed straight for the rocks as fast as his wings could carry him. As he got nearer, he saw the dragon family scrambling to the top of their sheltering rocks and heard the shouts of "Des! Des's back!" before their cries died away. He reached them, turned, and they stood in a line open-mouthed as Ben McIlwhinnie, looming over the line and the towers, reached out his huge hands, grasped the Strings in both fists, and snapped them as easily as blades of grass. A blinding flash lit the night sky, there was a loud bang, and before the shocked dragons could move, they saw Ben striding to the rescue towards them through the gap he had made.

Chapter 11

Ben the Hero

Gwen and Duncan, Emily and Tom stared open-mouthed as Ben approached, and Des looked at them all, enjoying their surprise. Emily recovered first.

"Ben! You're walking! I didn't think you'd wake until the Spring! However did you know we needed you?" Her voice wobbled.

"You must thank young Desmond's quick brain," said Ben. "And his loud voice!"

"We must thank YOU!" Gwen said in a trembling voice. "For coming to our rescue. Des, I never realised you meant to bring Ben! I thought you meant the others. However did you think of it?" Des beamed, but looked a bit embarrassed by all the admiration.

"But I fear there is no time to waste," Ben continued. "I have a feeling the Humans will be along to inspect the damage I caused to those Strings, and I really don't want to be seen, any more than you do. Climb on and we'll go."

"Find something to cling on to," Des advised them, as the children, followed by Duncan and finally Gwen and Lily, scrambled to find a secure perch on Ben's body. "Watch that wing, Duncan. OK everyone? It's a bit shoogly when he takes long strides. We'll be at the castle in no time, the speed he travels!"

"We need to be there before it gets light, I think," said Ben, setting off. "Is that possible?"

"Yes, no worries," said Des confidently. "Easy travelling until we're pretty close. Then we might have a bit of a hassle negotiating trees. You'll see when we get nearer." After the way Ben had solved the problem of the Singing Strings, he was sure he could cope with anything. He turned to Gwen. "Tell me how you managed without me yesterday. I thought those rocks would provide good shelter. Are you hungry? I brought some more food."

"We're OK."

"I found snails and berries and even a grouse!" Tom boasted. "And I lit the fire to cook it. We were starving."

"The children helped a lot."

"I kept a lookout all day!" said Emily proudly.

"Good for you!" said Des, still addressing Gwen.

"But you haven't heard the worst," said Duncan. "In the evening one of those Human flying machines came over. It was as close as I've ever seen. It made a deafening noise and a light shone down on us. It stayed for ages before it flew away."

"Hmm! Were you spotted?" asked Ben.

"I don't think so. Hard to be sure."

"That makes it more urgent to get away," said Ben, lengthening his stride. "If they have a flying machine, they will soon come to find out what has happened to those Strings of theirs. I had no idea Humans had learnt to fly! It must have happened while I was asleep. Hold tight, little dragons!"

For Tom and Emily, the rest of their journey was a magical adventure. With their tails wrapped securely round the small bushes and trees that had taken root during Ben's long sleep on the mountain, and clinging tight, they felt safe however uneven the ground was. The moon lit up the white land in front of them, the stars glittered overhead and they were higher than the treetops. They looked down on more herds of sleeping deer, giggled happily as Ben splashed through rivers, and half-listened to Des telling their parents of his journey and his rousing of Ben.

A sudden thought struck Emily. She was amazed she hadn't thought of it before. "What about our cave? Did it collapse when Ben stood up?"

Ben himself reassured her. "No, Emily, my chair is stronger than that! Your cave will still be there when you return. And I hope you WILL return! I have enjoyed more time awake since you youngsters arrived than I have for centuries."

"We'll be back. As soon as we can," Duncan promised. It was obvious that he regretted ever leaving! His wife said nothing. She was wondering how long broken wings took to mend.

"Will YOU go back, Ben?" Des asked. "Don't you want to keep walking now you've started? Once you've dropped us at the castle, you could go anywhere you like." He didn't add, "Can I come too...?" but Emily had a feeling he was thinking it.

"Ben you MUST come back!" she pleaded. "The glen wouldn't be the same without you."

Ben chuckled. "Oh, I shall return, as soon as I've seen you safe with your friends. I think I might be too visible in this wide country."

"You don't need to be frightened of Humans," said Tom. "You could squash them easily. They'd never try to put YOU in a cage, like they did to Ollie."

"That is true," said Ben. "But I would be visited and stared at and climbed on. They might even try to chip bits off me to take home! Humans seem to need to POSSESS things. They won't let things be! I would have no peace. I shall return to my glen. And when you come back you will find me guarding your cave as before."

Emily breathed a sigh of relief. "Oh good! It wouldn't seem like home without you. Don't look so disappointed, Des. You've still got your wings." Des laughed, then fell silent as he caught Duncan's scowl. It would be some time before Duncan had two good wings, and it seemed better not to rub it in.

They travelled on for some time, the silence broken only by Ben's humming as he strode along, and the occasional cry of a hunting owl. Then Des pointed ahead. "It's not too far now," he said. "Ben, there's a couple of Human houses close by, so veer left round the copse of trees ahead and then wade down that big river for a while. It's not too deep is it? When we leave the river, there's the trees to get through, but by then we're nearly there."

"Not a moment too soon!" said Duncan. "The moon's nearly down. We daren't be caught here in daylight."

"We'll get there. No worries!" said Des. "Here's the river."

"Hold tight!" said Ben as he took a mighty stride down the bank and into the water. It was deeper than the dragons expected, but still didn't reach Ben's knees. He strode down the middle, startling a colony of ducks which rose into the air with loud cries of alarm, and headed up river. Emily could see the Human house above the trees on the far bank, but it was dark and silent. She remembered waving to the girl called Phoebe on the seaside train, the one who had believed in dragons, and imagined that she was in that house, looking out of the window and seeing the huge head of Ben McIlwhinnie moving steadily past above the trees. Whatever would she think? Somehow that girl was a Human she would always remember and never be afraid of, however much her father warned her...

"Stop here, Ben!" Des's voice broke into her dreams. "See that wee gap in the trees on the far bank? That's the way to the castle. It's dead ahead, but you can't see it 'til you get close. This is where it gets tricky. You COULD smash your way through, but that would leave a trail that Humans could follow."

"And it would waste a lot of trees," Ben added. "Humans might do that, but I would rather not!"

"Right. So what do we do?"

"Hmmm." Ben was silent. Duncan gave a worried glance to the east, where the sky was lightening. They waited in suspense as Ben stood up tall and peered ahead over the barrier of the trees. "I see a large flat rock in the middle of the wood," he said at last. "Do you know the one I mean?"

"Yes."

"If I can reach that, could you get the dragons to the castle from there?"

"Yes. It's not too far to walk, Duncan. I'll fly ahead and alert the others, warn them you're injured and can't fly. Bring them to help."

"Then I think we have solved the problem. I will try to cause as little damage as I can. You dragons must hold tight."

Treading carefully, Ben approached the wood, and slowly passed between the trees at the edge, bending some with his huge hands to hold them out of his way. There were snowdrifts between the trees, but some places had been swept clear by the wind. Sometimes he edged sideways, holding his arms high. Tangled weeds and brambles were trodden underfoot but the dragons knew they would soon recover. A few saplings were damaged and branches snapped, but slowly and carefully, Ben made his way to towards the rock with the dragons clinging fast as twigs brushed past and threatened to dislodge them.

Des flew up. "Nearly there!" he shouted, and a moment later the rock came in sight; a huge grey boulder, rounded by time. The trees had grown around it so it would be hidden from Humans, unless they forced their way through the tangled woodland. Only flying dragons and huge giants would know it was there.

"Sweep the snow off the top, young dragons," said Ben, and waited, while everyone except Duncan set to work with tails. When it was clear, they watched as he lowered himself slowly onto his new seat.

"Thank you!" he said, heaving a deep sigh. "This is perfect. It solves the problem of how I am to get back. I can hardly walk all the way back in daylight without being seen. I was afraid I might have to lie down for the day, and I found it very difficult to rise again last time I did that! But here I can sit, and I don't think I will be visible above the trees. I can travel back overnight. After a snooze!" He beamed at them. "Off you go, young Desmond!"

"Can we go too?" Emily and Tom said together. "Please!"

Their parents agreed and they set off, following Des as he weaved his way through the trees. Suddenly their way was blocked by a high wire fence, obviously made by Humans. Emily had seen one like it when she and Dad had discovered the building site. It was a barrier for Humans, but no problem to a flying dragon. On the other side, half buried in scrubby bushes and dead grass, they could see a tumble-down Human house, missing part of its roof, with gaping holes in the walls and two broken chimneys standing up against the sky.

Further along the fence she could see a Human notice and Emily read: DANGER. FALLING MASONRY. KEEP OUT.

"Here we are! The famous Castle!" said Des and leading them over the fence, he swerved round the side of the ruin to land triumphantly on the top of a short flight of steps leading up to a huge dilapidated wooden door. A round hole had been huffed at the bottom to give the dragons a way in. Des pushed his way through, followed by Emily and Tom.

"I'm back!" he yelled into the echoing interior. "And look who's here!"

Chapter 12

Welcome to the Castle

Emily felt as though she had entered a dream. The inside of the castle was exactly like a picture in one of her books! A wide hall with stairs leading up into darkness, a slippery floor, marked in black and white squares, a dim empty passage ahead...

It was not empty for long! The echoes of Des's shout had hardly died away when there was a confused flurry of red and orange as Ollie and Alice burst through, waving their wings and cheering loudly. Alice rushed to give Emily a hug, and Ollie and Tom gave exultant High Fours. When Ellen and Oliver appeared, followed by Old George, everybody seemed to be talking at once.

Des shouted for quiet. "We've had a bit of a problem on the way here," he said, and the news produced a sudden hush. "An accident. Duncan has a broken wing. He and Gwen are still in the wood, with Lily. They're going to need some help."

"Right! Lead the way, Des," said Oliver.

"You can stay here with Georgie, can't you, George?" Ellen added, following them. "See you in a while kids. Show them around."

"We're coming too!" said Ollie indignantly, to Emily's relief. She wanted to show the others how they had travelled. There would be plenty of time to explore later. Tom guessed what she was thinking and agreed. "We'll all need to help," he said, winking at Emily.

Alice looked at them suspiciously. "Have you two got a secret?"

"Come and see!"

They squeezed through the hole one by one and flew over the fence following Des through the wood. Emily and Tom enjoyed the gasps of astonishment that greeted the huge seated figure of Ben

McIlwhinnie, with two dragons perched on his shoulder and Lily bouncing excitedly on his hand.

They gathered round Ben's feet, and tried to tell the story of the journey and the accident all at once. Ellen grasped the important fact out of the resulting jumble. "It's your wing that's gone, Duncan? We need to get you to the castle right away. George will see to it, don't worry. Gwen, you look frozen! Come along."

"We'll walk to the fence," said Oliver. "You'll not be able to fly over, but I expect we can melt a hole in it. Des, we'll need you too."

Gwen and Duncan climbed carefully down from Ben's shoulders and turned to face him. "Ben, you saved our lives, and we can never repay you," said Gwen with tears in her eyes.

"Oh, but you can!" Ben assured her. "You can come back to live in my cave. What would I do without your children to remind me that once I was young?"

"This wing will have to be fixed before I can fly again," said Duncan. "But as soon as it is, I promise I'll bring them all back to your cave. It's the best

127

home a dragon family could wish for. Good luck on your journey. And thank you!" Ben beamed at him and waved a huge hand as the grown-ups, with Lily scampering ahead, started slowly on foot towards the fence.

"Can we stay with Ben for a bit?" Alice called, and received a nod and wave from her mother as she disappeared. The four children flew up to Ben's knee, and Alice and Ollie told him and the others about their life in the castle. "It's not too bad, though I'd rather be at the camp," said Alice. "I still don't like sleeping inside. And we can't go out much because we might be seen by Humans. There are more of them round here, though they don't come near the castle. This wood's so thick I don't think they know it's there."

"Is old Ange still as much of a pain?" asked Tom.

"Sshh!" said Emily. "It's her place, and she's letting us stay. Better be a bit more polite."

"She did get a bit nicer when we went to rescue Ollie," Alice remarked, and even Ollie had to agree.

"I still keep out of her way when I can, though," he said. "It's a good thing the old ruin's so big."

Ben was looking down, listening to them with amusement, but suddenly he looked up. "I think I see someone coming," he said.

"Suffering Huffs, it's her!" said Ollie, and a moment later, Angelica herself landed beside them. She had left her emerald bag behind, but was still jangling with jewellery and sparkling with gold talons.

"Mr McIlwhinnie!" she exclaimed, ignoring the children. "Why are you sitting out here? I would be delighted to welcome you into my Castle."

Ben bowed his head gravely, but with a twinkle in his eye. "My dear Lady, I fear I would not fit! I will be very comfortable sitting here until it is time for me to go. I am enjoying hearing news from my young friends."

"Can I offer you some refreshment?" Angelica was putting on her very best voice, Emily thought!

"He likes Firewater!" Tom said, and Ben chuckled.

"Well remembered, young Tom! Indeed I do!"

"I will arrange it. Children, I think you should leave Mr McIlwhinnie to rest after his tiring journey. Don't pester him."

"Oh, I like their company. They are my very favourite dragons," said Ben fondly, and the children tried hard not to giggle at Angelica's expression. She could think of no response, so smiled sweetly. "Of course!" she said. "Goodbye. I am honoured to have met you." She bestowed a loving glance around and flew back towards the castle. The children burst out laughing as she disappeared.

"Good old Ange! She never changes," said Ollie. "At least she had the sense to be impressed with you, Ben!"

"Is she still flirting with Des?" asked Emily, remembering their first meeting.

"Yes. He's terrified!"

"I reckon it's the only thing he IS frightened of," added Ollie, and Ben joined their laughter, but then turned serious.

"Young Desmond is a most resourceful Dragon," he said. "It is well you had him with you in that blizzard. Leave me now – Tom and Emily need to eat and rest. They had no sleep last night! Come again at nightfall, before I leave for home."

"We will," Emily promised as they set off to fly back over the fence. On the way they passed a new dragon, grey with darker spikes, carrying a large jug of Firewater. "That's Harold," said Alice. "He and his wife Maggie have lived with Auntie Ange for years, helping out and things. They're nice."

They reached the old house and scrambled through the door one by one. "Drink first, then we'll show you around," said Ollie, leading the way along the passage to a big room with a stone floor. There was no glass in the window, but a wood fire burned underneath it, so that the smoke drifted out, and sometimes blew back in. Dragons can stand a good deal of smoke, so Emily and Tom felt at home straight away. "Humans used to use that place for fires, we think," said Ollie, pointing, "but Dad said if smoke came out of that tower-thing up on the roof it would most likely be spotted."

An elderly dragon, pale grey with wings almost pure white, was stirring a pot on the fire, and Alice introduced Emily and Tom. She looked pleased to see them, to Emily's relief, and ladled mugs of hot ginger fizz. Ellen came in while they were drinking it.

"How's Dad?" Emily asked at once.

"He'll be fine. George is strapping up his wing now. It still hurts. It's a good thing you kids were out. He swore quite a lot while it was being fixed! Maggie, can we cope with all these children?"

"Och, I can find plenty of jobs for them to do!" said old Maggie, smiling.

"When we've shown them round," said Ollie hurriedly, finishing his fizz in a big gulp. "Come on you two."

The four of them thanked Maggie, and Ollie and Alice led the way out of the big room. Emily remembered that this was called a 'kitchen', and Alice agreed. "There's another big room across here," she said, leading them across the passage. It was almost intact, though missing glass from big windows that looked onto a tangle of bushes and a hummocky slope of snow. They could see the fence at the end of the slope, and the thick wood beyond it. To Emily's amazement there was even some Human furniture. Alice pointed to a long couch with a high back. It was battered and faded, but had once been red and gold. "That's Angie's," she said.

"The floor isn't good enough for her!" said Ollie. "She drapes herself along that and tries to issue orders. Drives us all mad when she's in her Lady of the Castle mood."

"Wait 'til you see where she sleeps!" Alice added, leading them upstairs. There were bits of broken post on the way up. "Shouldn't there be a line of sticks and a sloping rail thing?" Emily asked Alice as they climbed, remembering pictures she had seen.

"Burnt for firewood long ago, I expect," said Alice. "Most of the rooms up here have holes in their roofs, but look at this one!" Emily gasped. Inside the room was a huge bed with a tattered canopy, and other pieces of wooden furniture stood against the walls. "I guess this is where Angie sleeps," she said. "No wonder she thinks she's a Lady!"

Tom scampered across the room and took a flying leap onto the bed. "Great for bouncing!" he said, raising clouds of dust. "Is there one of these for us?"

133

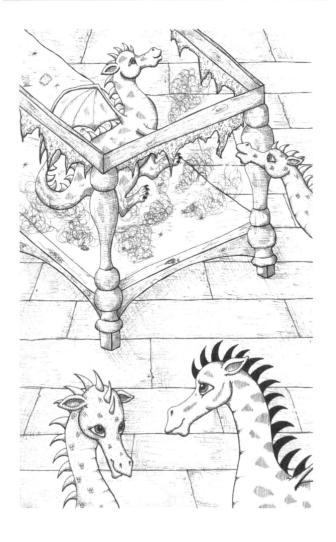

"No chance!" said Ollie. "There are a few smaller ones, but the grown-ups have got them. Maggie and Harold's room has one, and a decent roof too – it's along there. Mum and Dad sleep up here too – not in there, though!" They had passed a room with a hole in the roof and a large snowdrift on the floor. "I guess they'll find somewhere decent for your folks, and you two can join us in the cellar. Wait 'til you see that!"

"Grandad has a nice wee room," added Alice. "It's the only one that still has glass in the window, so it's cosy. He had a nasty cough when we first arrived, but it's a bit better now. Maggie's always trying to feed him up!"

They finished exploring upstairs, launched themselves off the platform at the top and landed in the hall. Then Ollie led the way through a battered door and down a steep flight of stone stairs to a dim cellar below the kitchen. It had an arched roof and several smaller rooms, with tiny high windows, leading off. Inside were stores of food and piles of soft sweet-smelling dried grass. "That's Humans' hay," Alice said. "There's no heather round here, so we use this instead. And straw, which is spikier, but OK underneath. You can go out at night and collect what's left in the fields. Des collected lots when he brought Angie and Grandad back. We'll make beds for you. He has one in the very top of the bit of the house that's still standing. It has windows all round, so he says he can keep watch for Humans from there."

"And it keeps him well away from Ange!" Ollie added.

They were adding new beds in Alice and Ollie's rooms when there was a shout from the top of their stairs.

"Food at last!" said Ollie, and led the dash to the kitchen.

Chapter 13

Settling In

Everyone gathered in the big kitchen, which seemed much smaller when it was so full of dragons. Georgie and Lily were already sitting together, sharing a bowl of Maggie's pigeon and tattie stew. Duncan's wing had been strapped up by Old George, who assured him it would mend as good as new, but only if he didn't try to fly for a few weeks.

"Great!" said Ollie, through mouthfuls of stew. "That means you'll have to stay 'til it's better."

"And 'til there's a thaw," added Ellen. "There's no sign of one at the moment."

"It's very kind of you to have us all to stay," Gwen added to Angelica. "Are you sure that's all right? I couldn't even bring much food with me."

"I brought some!" said Des, flourishing the bag that nobody had noticed in the hustle of their arrival. "I found the bumblebugs, Gwen. Wouldn't want them to go to waste!"

"Trust you!" said Duncan.

Angelica took a deep breath and was preparing to make a gracious speech, but old Maggie got in first.

"Of course you can stay!" she said. "We've got plenty of food stored down in the cellar, and I know everybody will help. It's lovely to have new company. Isn't it, Harold?" The silent Harold nodded with his mouth full. "And it will keep the children happy. Young Alice has been moping for her friend, haven't you, dear?"

"And it's SUCH a relief to know that your darling golden baby is safe," Angelica added. Gwen smiled back warily. She had never quite trusted Angelica's fondness for Lily!

"It's starting to snow again," said Des as a flurry of fat flakes drifted through the open window and sizzled as they hit the fire.

"I hope Ben won't get lost on his way home," said Tom.

Des laughed. "He'll follow his own footprints! He left a huge trail of them. I'd love to know what the Humans are thinking. They can hardly have missed them if they've come to mend the break in their Strings."

"They lead right here!" Duncan sounded worried. "I hope we haven't brought danger with us."

"The trail stopped at the river further down," Des reminded him.

"Close, but not too dangerous," Oliver said. "We'll check for tracks when we go to see Ben off. The good thing about this snow is that we can see if Humans have been around. And so far they haven't come any nearer than the big pond near the edge of this wood. They seem to like sliding about on it for some reason. Isn't that right Des?"

Des, who was accepting a third helping of stew from Maggie, nodded. "I keep a good look-out from my tower, and no one's come anywhere near," he said.

"Have you heard one of their horrible flying machines?" asked Gwen. "One of them hovered above us, shining a light, when we were hiding in the valley of the Singing Strings. Just before Ben and Des came to find us. If one comes near here it might be dangerous. It could fly over that fence!"

"Never heard one over here," said Harold, shaking his head.

"It's worth remembering," said Oliver. "We don't want to leave traces of ourselves just in case. Kids, weren't you lying in the snow outside making patterns yesterday?"

"Yes. Georgie too," admitted Alice. "A whole line of them."

"A line of flying dragons!" said Des. "I saw them from the tower. Any new snow will cover them, though, no worries. Why don't you two come up and see them before they disappear?" he added, getting up and giving old Maggie a hug. "Great stew, Mags! We'll help clear up next time, OK?" It was obvious that Des could twist Maggie round his claw, Emily thought, amused, as she followed the others up two flights of stairs to the small square tower room almost filled with Des's straw and hay bed.

Looking out of the South window, over the smoothest stretch of snow inside the fence, they could clearly see that Alice, Ollie and Georgie had spent some time making dragon patterns by lying down in the snow and spreading their wings wide. "Even better than the patterns we made on the beach, the ones that girl recognised," said Emily.

"We can rough them up now you've seen them," said Alice. "Looks like the snow's stopping again."

The windows faced in four directions, giving a wide view. "Isn't that a Human house over there?" asked Tom, leaning out. "Dad'll think that's a bit too close!"

"There's a window high up," said Emily, peering over his wings. "Do you think Humans could see us from there if they looked out?"

"No, too far away," said Des. "Tell you what I CAN see, though: Ben's bald head! Look!"

They crowded to the North window and rising above the trees was the familiar domed shape.

"Good thing it's only the top of his head. Could be anything. But he's going tonight, so shouldn't be any problem. Why don't you lot go outside for a look around while it's not snowing. Then I can catch up on some sleep before we say goodbye to Ben."

The children rushed down the stairs, through the front door and out into the garden, where they threw snowballs energetically on the open area, ruining the dragon prints in the process. Then they made their way round the fence on the inside, discovering tangled shrubs, a small iced-over pond, the remains of a battered garden shed, some ruined outbuildings and a hole in the wire that had been melted for Duncan to get through.

"It's a good thing this outside bit's a decent size..." Ollie began.

"It's a garden," Emily, the reader of Human books, interrupted.

"I keep telling him," Alice sighed.

"As I was saying.... because we're not often allowed outside the fence. Old Ange is terrified that with so many of us here, someone will be spotted. She likes her old castle and wants to stay."

"She'd like Grandad to stay permanently," said Alice, rather sadly.

"But I reckon she'll be fed up with the rest of us by the time winter's over," said Ollie. "Good thing too. I like freedom. I want to go back to your place."

"Well, we're stuck here until Dad's wing's better," said Emily.

"Good, because it's much more fun now you're here," said Alice. "Ollie and I were beginning to fight. I don't think I could have coped with him for much longer! "

"We need to get some Tail-Stane going," said Tom eagerly. He had been trying to bring the subject up for some time, despite his disappointment over the size of the little pond. He started to expound the joys of the game to Ollie, while Alice and Emily went back inside to see if it was time to fly out and say goodbye to Ben. Emily, who had been awake for a long time, was beginning to think longingly of her new bed.

Oliver agreed that they could go, and George was getting ready to accompany them, when the boys rushed past and up the stairs. "Ollie's thought of something!" Tom shouted as he ran.

"They can follow," said Alice, and led the way over the fence and through the wood to the place where Ben was sitting, eyes closed, dozing. He woke as they landed in front of him, and was particularly pleased to see his old friend, George. He chuckled as he pictured them all collected in the kitchen eating Maggie's stew. "A true Conflagration of Dragons!" he said. "And have you mended Duncan's wing for him? Good. He must make certain it is healed before he attempts to travel back to my glen. I might not be so easy to wake a second time."

The boys and the rest of the family arrived, and between them they told of their plans for the rest of the winter, promising to return as soon as they could. "We'll creep back quietly, so as not to wake you," Gwen promised and Ben chuckled again.

"You will have lots of news, and I shall want to hear it!" he said. "Go back to your castle now. Young

Emily needs a sleep, by the look of her. I will leave at nightfall and be back on my chair by sun-up. Stay safe, young Dragons! Goodbye until we meet again."

Des, the last to leave, had a final thought. "Ben, what if the Humans have mended those Strings? Mind you don't hit them in the dark!"

"If they have been mended, I will snap them again. No worries, as you are fond of saying. Look after my young friends, Desmond. And well done! You have been a true hero." He smiled as Des, looking pleased but a little embarrassed, gave a final wave and disappeared after the others. Dusk was falling; it would soon be time to for him to depart.

At the top window of the Human house across the forest, two children peered through the gathering dusk. "See it?" said the smaller one. "A huge whiteish dome-thing in the middle of the trees. I've never seen it before, have you? Got the binoculars?"

"Aliens have landed!" joked the second, focussing and peering closely. "Getting too dark to see properly, but you're right, there is *something* there. No wee green Martians, though. Have a look." She passed the binoculars over. "It *is* kind of flying-saucer-shaped, isn't it? Let's ring the others and go and see if we can find it in the morning. I hope we get the power back soon. I've only just enough phone battery left."

"It's not far from that old ruin we've been warned about, but we don't need to tell anyone we're heading that way."

They grinned conspiratorially as they headed downstairs.

Chapter 14

Grounded!

Supper was early, but Emily was too tired to enjoy it, and took herself straight to bed after she had eaten. Alice promised to creep down later. Tom tried to keep awake, but soon he drooped too and followed. The cellar room he was to share with Ollie seemed very dark and creepy, even to a cave-dweller, and when he woke a little later, wondering where he was, he was relieved to hear Ollie snoring softly by the far wall.

After breakfast next day, the grown-ups gathered them together and laid down the law.

"This is a good place Angie's found," Oliver admitted, a little reluctantly, "but it's a bit close to Humans for comfort. The high fence keeps them out, but it wouldn't stop them for long if they knew we were here. It was easy for three dragons to stay hidden, but with so many of us here now, we have to be VERY careful. A sighting of even one of us might bring snoopers around."

"I do hope we haven't left too many tracks in the snow," Gwen worried. "I think our coming has put you in greater danger."

"You HAD to come!" said Ellen. "And you can't leave for several weeks. So we just have to be careful. Oliver and I went out last night to check that Ben had left safely. We went as far as the river, and swept all our tracks away on the way back. So I think we're safe for the present."

"Now we have to stay that way," said Oliver sternly. "We stay inside as much as possible. Kids, you don't go beyond the fence. Understand?"

"Not EVER?" Ollie was outraged.

"Sorry, not ever. There's plenty of room to play in the.... what do you call it, Alice?"

"Garden."

"Yes – and you can roam all over the place inside," Ellen continued. There was a meaningful cough from

Angelica. "Not in your aunt's room, obviously, or Maggie and Harold's, but everywhere else."

"Any foraging will be done at night, and only by Des and another of us," Oliver concluded. "Agreed, Des?"

The children stared hard at Des, willing him to disagree, but he nodded his head. "Yes, you're right. A big group like this is dodgy. That's one of the reasons I travel solo. Sorry kids, you'll need to stick to the rules."

"Even Des sees the sense of it!" Duncan added firmly, looking at the four mutinous faces. "In fact, since I'm not much use for anything much with this wretched wing, I'll offer to keep a good look-out from Des's tower whenever the kids are outside. I can give warning to hide if there's any sign of Humans around."

"Good idea!" said Oliver. The children sighed, seeing another small bit of freedom disappearing. They round looked at the resolute expressions of the grown-ups. Only Old George looked sympathetic, but even he was shaking his head at them. Des gave a rueful shrug at Ollie's glare.

"There's a bitter wind getting up, blowing the snow around," he said, sounding apologetic. "Why don't you find a place to play Tom's Tail-Stane game inside? I'll join you in a while."

The four children turned and headed out of the kitchen, too fed up to argue. Even Des had ranged himself against them! "I reckon he's getting old," Ollie muttered in disgust.

"This is worse than home!" Tom said.

"You argued that we should come," Emily reminded him.

"Yeah, well...." Tom kicked at the first stair in the hallway moodily.

"Is this place big enough for your game, Tom?" asked Alice, trying to cheer up the gloom.

"Not really, but I suppose it'll have to do."

"Where will we find stones? The garden's covered with snow."

"No problem. Ollie found something! Wait here!" Tom dashed away down the cellar stairs, looking a bit more cheerful. The others gathered in a huddle.

"Not good!" said Alice.

"No. There is something they don't know about, though," said Ollie, thoughtfully. "Tell you later," he added as Tom rushed back, carrying a small and grubby yellow ball.

"Ollie found a couple of these in one of the rooms upstairs. We could use it instead of stones, even when we play outside, as there isn't any decent ice round here. OK, this is what you do!"

For most of the morning, Tom and Emily demonstrated the techniques involved in Tail-Stane and they invented some rules of play that fitted the space in the hall. After the ball had flown once through the hole in the door and three times through a broken window, they blocked the holes with pieces of wood lying around the cellar. They devised a points system for teams, after much arguing. After a while Des joined them and play grew more boisterous. Angelica, looking particularly martyred, disappeared upstairs and firmly shut her door. A spectacularly fine shot by Tom sent the ball halfway up the stairs after her, and they worked out how to use the upstairs space as well, for 'Tall-Tail-Stane' as Tom christened it, scoring 'uppers and dooners'.

They were feeling a good deal more cheerful as they streamed into the kitchen for drinks.

"I suppose you got rid of Ange for us, but I wish there was somewhere else for you to play," Ellen said wearily.

"Isn't there room in that cellar of yours?" Gwen was obviously still feeling a little guilty at inflicting her family on the castle. "Here, take some bumble-bugs with you."

"Suppose we could check," said Ollie, heading out of the door. "Just us four," he added pointedly to Des, who had followed them. Des held up his talons in surrender.

"Fine. Whatever you're up to, I don't want to know!" he said. He looked a little hurt, so Emily gave him a bumblebug before she followed the others and was rewarded with a wink as he went back into the kitchen to join the grown-ups.

Safely inside the boys' bedroom, the four slumped moodily on the hay. The excitement of Tail-Stane had fizzled out. "I can't believe Des joined the grown-up side!" Ollie complained. "I knew Mum and Dad were worried, but I thought he'd help us to get out *sometimes*."

"You can't really blame them," said the reasonable Alice, "We nearly lost you to a zoo, remember?"

"If Humans came here, we could gang together and kill them," Tom argued. "Lots of flaming Huff, no problem!"

"Not sure that would help us stay hidden!" said Emily. She wanted to support Alice, but felt as frustrated as the boys. Being trapped in the cave at home had been bad enough!

"There's one thing we've found out that nobody else knows about," said Ollie. "It might be just what we need. Right Allie?" Alice nodded, and they leaned their heads together as he lowered his voice. But just as he was about to tell them, a shout of "Lunch" from above stopped him. "Tell you later," he said, heading upstairs, leaving Tom and Emily in suspense.

This time there were four Human children craning out of the top window.

"There's nothing there," said a new one.

"I TOLD you!" said the first. "It WAS there, last night – we both saw it – and now it's gone. Flown away. MUST have been a UFO. Huge and domed, honestly... Wasn't it, Lisa?"

"OK, OK, we'll go and investigate," said the tallest of the four. "I'm fed up stuck inside with the power off again. It's snowing, but we can put on waterproofs and it'll be more sheltered in the woods. Let's get going."

"What were you going to tell us?" Emily asked some time later, after they had helped to clear up after lunch and were heading back to the cellar.

Ollie led them to the far end, past their bedrooms, and showed a heap of broken wood and rubbish. "It's behind here," he said. "We found it when we were collecting up some firewood, didn't we, Allie? There's a door and a bit of passage, and then another door. It leads to one of those broken-down buildings outside."

"And from there into the garden," added Alice. "The back bit...."

"The bit that can't be seen from the tower!" Ollie finished, triumphantly. "No use for everyday, but very handy to know about in case of need. Makes me feel much less trapped. Come on, we'll show you."

They squeezed through the door and set off slowly down the narrow passage in single file. Ollie sent up a Huff which lit up ancient cobwebs and caused a scuttle of spiders on the roof. He was just about to turn a corner when he stopped so abruptly that Tom tripped over the end of his tail.

"What is it?" whispered Alice from the rear.

"Thought I heard something."

They froze, and in the silence heard an unmistakeable scuffle.

"Back," whispered Ollie. They reversed awkwardly in the narrow passage and Alice led the way back to the cellar. They stood in silence, listening hard. "It can't be the parents, surely!" Ollie moaned.

Then they heard it again. It sounded like stealthy footsteps.

"Could be Des. It would be just like him! Trying to give us a fright." Emily was trying to reassure herself as well as the others.

The footsteps stopped, and the dragons held their breath, so not even smoke could give them away. After a few seconds that felt like hours, they heard them again.

"Hide behind the heap," Ollie mouthed to Emily and Alice and pulled Tom back against the wall. "See which of them it is, then pounce!

Chapter 15

Strange Meeting

The four dragons hardly dared to breathe in the darkness. Emily could feel Alice quivering with excitement. They couldn't see the boys. It seemed a long time before the stealthy footsteps came again, and then a thin beam of light came from the open door. It flashed round, fortunately missing the dragons, and she heard a faint "Wow!" Another beam, and then more footsteps. Alice breathed "Humans!" in Emily's ear and they froze in horror. The dreaded Humans were close enough to touch! Their hideout was discovered.

Ollie was even more horrified. He had experienced Humans at first hand, and it still gave him nightmares. He knew how rough and dangerous they could be. He couldn't let them find the stairs into the rest of the house, and discover everyone in the kitchen. Sudden attack was the only thing to do. Pushing Tom behind him he sent a furious spurt of flame towards the ceiling.

The cellar lit up. Alice, guessing the danger, scampered round the Humans and stood on guard at the bottom of the stairs. Her flaming Huff joined Ollie's and in the sudden bright light they saw their enemies clearly.

Emily gasped. Her books had been brought to life! Two girls and two boys – just like in all the stories! They were not very old, all wearing bright jackets, woolly hats, scarves and gloves. They looked terrified as Ollie reared up and huffed again, looking bigger and redder than usual in the flickering light.

"It's the aliens from that spaceship!" the smallest one whispered.

"No, it's not! They're dragons!" said a girl.

"Blue ones?" asked a smaller girl dubiously, looking from Tom to Emily.

"WHY NOT?" said Tom indignantly, producing a small flame. The four children backed away.

"You can *talk?*"

"Of course we can," said Ollie fiercely. "We can fly as well. We can fight and breathe fire. *And we don't like Humans!*" he added in a dangerous hissing whisper, dropping to all fours and glaring at the huddle of children.

"I don't much like what I've heard about dragons either," said the bigger girl bravely, as the smaller two hid behind her. "But I thought you were just creatures in old stories. Wow! I can't wait to tell everyone you're REAL!"

"Yeah, it's a major scientific discovery! Are there any more of you?" that was the bigger boy, who was looking more excited than frightened.

"Lots!" said Ollie, grimly. "Much bigger ones! You won't be escaping to tell ANYONE." He advanced another step towards them, breathing more fire and Emily saw the smallest child reach for a comforting hand. She knew they were dangerous creatures, but it was difficult not to feel sorry for the little one.

"You can't keep us here! People will come looking for us!"

"There won't be anything left to find..." Ollie, grinning and showing his teeth, was looking more terrifying by the minute, Alice thought. She decided to intervene before he did anything stupid.

"How did you get in?" she demanded.

"We found a wee hole in the fence," the larger boy said. "We live on the other side of the wood. We don't often come here, because we've never been able to get over the fence to explore this old ruin before."

"I suppose it's easy for you. You can fly over!" said the first girl. "This is amazing! Have you lived here long? Honestly, we don't want to harm you!"

"I'd like to see you try!" Ollie laughed scornfully.

"Yeah!" Tom agreed, moving closer since Ollie seemed to have the upper hand.

Alice moved in as well. "*We* don't want to harm *you*," she said, "but we can't let you go away and tell other Humans that we're here."

"Why not? They'd be really interested...."

"And what would they do when they found out?" Ollie interrupted. "I'll tell you! They'd come here and capture us. Knock us out. Put us in cages. Sell us to zoos. Trust me, I know what Humans are like..." He was shaking now, Emily realised, not sure whether it was fury or fear. His recent experience of capture and imprisonment was obviously still vivid in his mind.

She had been guarding the entrance to the passage, behind the children, but now she came forward. "They're right," she said. "Nobody else must know about this. If OUR parents found out we'd be in real trouble. We'd have to move somewhere else and that would put us in more danger. And I bet YOUR parents would be furious if they found out you'd ignored that notice and come through the fence. You'd better keep quiet about this place. And us!"

"If all our grown-ups banded together they might attack your house and burn it down," Ollie said. "They could, easily!"

"So it would be better for everyone if we ALL kept quiet," Alice concluded, firmly. "What do you say?"

There was another tense silence. The dragons stayed motionless, but the children looked at each other doubtfully. Finally the small boy burst out. "I think we should be friends. I want to know about that flying saucer we saw. Did you land in it? Where has it gone?"

The dragons looked at each other, bemused. "Flying what?" said Tom, but before anyone could explain what a flying saucer was, a new voice broke in.

"Suffering Huffs, what are you lot LIKE?! Letting Humans in! What are you PLAYING at...?"

It was Des, standing on the stairs, wings outstretched. He looked huge and menacing, and sent a great spurt of flame to the cellar roof. The four children shrank back, shielding their eyes, the younger girl letting out a stifled scream. Emily hardly recognised this new fierce Desmond. "It's all right...." she began as the flare died, but Ollie ignored her and turned on Des furiously.

"Don't blame us! Who left that hole in the fence you made for Dad to get through? That's how *they* got in! And we're sorting it ourselves, so GET LOST!" Des pretended to shrink back. It was obvious that he couldn't decide whether to laugh or attack! Emily decided to intervene.

"Honestly, Des, we ARE sorting it. They'll not tell anybody about us. You mustn't tell the parents. Promise?"

Des let out another sizeable huff, which caused further panic among the children. "Right, right, the problem's all yours!" he said. "Just get it sorted. I DON'T WANT TO KNOW!"

He turned and pushed open the door. "Yell if you need help," he added over his shoulder. There were sighs of relief all round as the red spike at the end of his tail disappeared.

"Phew! He looked really dangerous. I thought we'd had it!" said the bigger boy.

"He isn't really...." Alice began, but Ollie interrupted again.

"Yeah, he can be pretty savage when he wants to be. You don't want to mess with ANY of our grownups. Or me, come to that!"

There was another tense silence.

"Look, why don't we all go into our room and sit down and discuss what to do," Alice the Peacemaker suggested, looking round "Let's promise not to attack each other. The damage is done now – you've seen us. We've never actually met Humans before, though we've spied on you lots of times. That OK with you, Ollie?"

Ollie shrugged. "There are only two options. We trust that you won't give us away. Or we have to kill you. Better start talking."

Emily led the way and the four children and three dragons settled on the straw and hay beds. Ollie came last and stood guard in front of the doorway. He certainly wasn't prepared to relax in the company of Humans, even small ones.

Tom broke the slightly awkward pause. "What was all that stuff about a flying saucer?" he asked.

"I thought you might have landed in it," the wee boy said. "I spotted it from the window. Lisa saw it too. A huge white dome-thing in the wood. A space ship, I think. But the next morning it had flown away. Was it yours?"

Tom started to laugh. "That must have been...." he started, but Emily cut him off. "We didn't see anything," she said, giving Tom a sharp prod with her tail. "But we didn't come in a space ship. We're from a glen up north. We're here because of the snow."

"It's great isn't it?" said the bigger girl. "All the schools are closed. My name's Lisa, by the way. This is Megan, and they're Finn and Charlie. Do you have names?" Alice introduced them, wishing that Ollie would stop glowering.

"Why are you different colours?" Finn wanted to know, and Emily explained that English dragons are usually red, whereas Scottish dragons are blue.

"What about that huge fierce dragon?" Megan said. "He seemed to be lots of colours. He was horrible!"

Ollie laughed scornfully. "You think he's huge?" he said. "Wait 'til you see my Dad. And theirs. Des is just a bigger kid, that's all."

"He isn't really horrible," said Alice, glaring at Ollie. "He paints his wings and spikes. He comes from Wales so he's green, underneath the painted bits, but he's travelled all over the place." Her voice trailed off.

166

"He's called Des," Emily added, trying to help Alice break the tension that Ollie was creating by looming in the doorway. "He painted our spikes for us. He did Ollie's black! We think he's brilliant."

Lisa smiled, beginning to relax. "Would you like a humbug?" she asked, offering a paper bag with stripy sweets inside. Tom grinned. "They're like our bumblebugs!" he said. "Taste different though," he added, crunching hard. Alice and Emily accepted too, but Ollie feeling things were getting much too friendly, declined. He brought the subject back to their big problem.

"You do understand, don't you?" he said, sounding very determined. "Keeping ourselves secret from Humans is a matter of life and death for us. It isn't a joke. I've been shut in a cage, so I know what I'm talking about. These three haven't. I have to be sure you won't tell ANYBODY that we're here. Otherwise I can't let you go. I know Des would agree with me, and he's waiting upstairs. One call from us and he'll be back. With our Dads."

"Oh, Ollie...." Alice began, but Lisa and Finn looked at each other, obviously worried. Finn nodded and Lisa leaned forward earnestly.

"We do understand, honestly! I know how cruel some people can be. We've done projects on endangered species, and had debates about keeping animals in zoos. It must be hard for you, having to keep yourselves hidden all the time. If you let us go," she looked steadily at Ollie, "all four of us will swear to tell nobody where we've been, and we'll try to forget we ever saw you. You can trust us." She smiled ruefully. "I'd love to take a photo of us all, just to keep as a souvenir, but I suppose that would be too dangerous, wouldn't it?"

"Of course it would!" said Ollie. "And how do you know you haven't been followed? I bet you've left footprints in the snow, so anyone else can see where you've been."

"Noone knows we were coming here. They can't have followed us!" said Lisa.

"We must have left footprints though," Finn admitted. "Can we just creep out the way we came in? Then we can scuff them up."

"That would help," said Alice, glancing hopefully at Ollie.

"And what if Duncan's on watch in the tower room? If we're to let you go, we can't let him see you. So it's not that easy, is it!"

Chapter 16

Friends in Secret

All eight of them thought for a few minutes in silence. "We could wait until it's dark," Emily suggested.

Finn glanced at something strapped round his wrist. "No we can't. There'd be a search party out looking for us. We're a bit late already. We need to go as soon as we can. The parents get really het up if we're out after dark."

"Ours do too!" said Emily, remembering the trouble there had been over their trip to the old cave in the autumn.

"Could we fly them out?" Alice suggested doubtfully, looking at Ollie. "Des might help..." Despite her worry, Emily almost laughed at the horror on Lisa's face and the excited grin on little Charlie's.

Ollie ignored the suggestion. He had been thinking hard, and now issued orders. "Tom, scoot upstairs and check on the parents. Make sure that Duncan's in the kitchen. If he isn't, try to get him down somehow. Ask Maggie for some biscuits or something and say we're busy down here. Quick as you can, but act casual! Don't look all guilty if you see Des." Tom nodded and dashed away.

"Right – you!" he pointed to Finn, "Come through the passage with me and we'll see if we can get you to the hole in the fence without being seen. You others wait here. And keep quiet. Allie and Em, hide them in the hay if you hear someone coming down the stairs." He shoved Finn ahead of him and they disappeared round the corner.

Without Ollie the atmosphere relaxed. "I've read stories about dragons," Megan said, "but I NEVER thought I'd meet one! You're MUCH nicer than dragons in books. I think you're a lovely colour, Emily. Let me see your wings spread out."

"Alice and I have read books about Humans!" said Emily, spreading her wings for Megan to admire,

171

while Alice showed Lisa her painted spikes. "When you came into our cellar it was EXACTLY like one of our stories. The children in them are always finding tunnels and passages and things."

"Can you read as well?" Lisa sounded amazed.

"We girls can, can't we, Alice?"

"Where do you get books from?"

"I got mine from my Gran. She taught Mum to read, and Mum taught me. Not all dragons can read, but it's great in winter if you're shut inside. I like to read in bed."

Lisa smiled. "Me too!"

"Dad found some when he went foraging one time. They had been left in a bin somewhere. Emily and I share. Those are mine." Alice pointed to three battered books tucked under her bed.

Tom rushed back in, clutching four blackened bramble biscuits in one talon, and the Tail-Stane ball in the other. "I asked Maggie for two each, so we could share, but she said we wouldn't eat our supper," he said, breathlessly. "Sorry!"

"That's all right. She sounds just like our Mum," said Megan.

Lisa peered at the biscuits. "Do you *like* them black like that?" she asked curiously.

"We like things burnt and crunchy," Emily explained. "All dragons do."

Tom held the ball out to Charlie. "We found this in a room upstairs," he said. "What do you call it?"

"It's a tennis ball."

"What's tennis?" The two boys went into a huddle and could be heard explaining the rules of tennis, football and tail-stane, demonstrating with waving arms, tails, legs and wings.

"Can you tell me something?" said Emily. She rummaged beside her bed and found the small elastic band with the shiny pink bobbles that she had picked up in her old cave on their secret expedition in the autumn. "What's this?" She held it out to Lisa.

"It's a hair bobble!" said Lisa. "Look! This is how we wear them." She pulled off her woolly hat and turned round. Her thick fair hair was tied back with a similar one. "You could wear that round your wrist like a bracelet!" She pulled her blue one off and held it out to Alice. "Would you like one too? It matches your spikes! It could be a kind of token of friendship, and a pledge that we won't tell!" Alice beamed, and she and Emily held out their talons so that Lisa could fix the bobbles. They were admiring them with Megan when they heard Ollie and Finn returning. They tried to hide the bobbles and Lisa bundled her hair back inside her hat.

"All clear, Tom?" asked Ollie. Tom emerged reluctantly from his discussion of Tail-Stane.

"Yes, Dad's in the kitchen. They're all sitting round having tea. Except Ange. Don't know where she is."

"She can't see the back from her room. Right. Let's go. Quiet as you can."

They crept in single file across the cellar and through the passage. Lisa and Emily came last. "I wish we could come back!" Lisa whispered, and Emily nodded. "So do I. I'd like to be friends. There's lots I'd love to talk about. And I'd like you to see my wee sister. She's gold and really cute. But it's no good. It's just too dangerous!"

Out in the garden the snow had started falling again. "Good," said Ollie, "it'll help cover your tracks." He led the way round the dilapidated outbuildings and in a corner they could see the hole that had been huffed in the fence. On the other side was a jumble of human footprints.

"Right, out you go," said Ollie. "And remember; we know where you live, and *we breathe fire!*"

"You don't need to worry," said Lisa, facing him bravely. "We've all promised. We'll say nothing to anybody. You're quite safe." The four of them nodded, and Charlie solemnly held up his right hand.

"Swear properly!" he told the others. They stood in a row and chanted "We swear!" in whispered unison.

"We believe you," Alice assured them.

One by one, the four children squeezed through the hole in the fence.

"Good luck, and thanks," said Finn, and the others nodded. Charlie gave Tom cheerful grin. "Bye," said Megan, looking quite tearful. "Stay safe!" Lisa said solemnly as she too turned to go.

"Cover your tracks!" said Ollie, and as they trudged away through the snow, Lisa and Finn scuffed their footprints. Lisa turned and waved before they disappeared into the trees. Emily waved back. She suddenly remembered waving to the girl on the train back in the summer – a wave she had not even told Alice about. Two girls she knew she would not see again. "Phoebe and Lisa," she said to herself. "I wish we could all be friends!"

Ollie turned back to the door, and he and Tom rubbed the humans' footprints with their tails as they went. "Good thing the hole in the fence wasn't over there," Tom said, cheerfully, pointing across the garden. "Four sets of footprints across that bit would have taken some explaining! Hey, I've got lots of new ideas for Tail-Stane from that wee Charlie guy…" He disappeared into the passage with Ollie.

Emily and Alice looked at each other. "That was fantastic!" Alice said. "I wish they could have stayed longer. I hope that little Charlie doesn't forget and tell. I think we can trust Lisa and Finn and Megan."

"I'd love to see them again," said Emily with a sigh.

"Me too," said Alice. "And I think they felt the same."

They followed the boys through the passage and into the cellar. "Suffering Huffs that was close!" said Ollie. "I think we've got away with it, as long as we can trust them."

"I'm sure we can!" said Emily.

"I know you are," said Ollie, "I wish I was!"

"Hi, you lot!" Des gave a low call from the stairs.

"You can come down," Alice called.

Des bounded down into the cellar. "No stow-aways? Good. Close call, that. Might not be the end of it, either."

"Yes it will!" said Emily firmly. "We explained to them how dangerous it is for dragons, and they promised to keep our secret. We trust them." Alice and Tom nodded their agreement. Des looked at Ollie.

"I *think* I do," he said slowly. "They seemed quite decent. They were terrified of you, Des!"

"So was I!" Alice interrupted.

"And I added bits about fire-breathing and huge fierce grown-ups and knowing where their house was. I didn't get too friendly."

"They were a bit frightened of *you* as well," Tom grinned.

"Well done, mate," said Des to Ollie. "But I'll keep a keen look-out from the tower for a few days, just in case. Now, have they left tracks?"

"We scuffed out the ones in the garden."

"And they were covering their own tracks on the way home," added Alice, still determined to believe the best of their visitors.

"I'll fly out and check around. I hope they didn't spot Ben yesterday,"

"They did!" Emily exclaimed. "That's why they came. They saw his bald head and thought a space ship had landed. Tom nearly gave the game away."

Tom scowled at her, but the rest laughed. "Brilliant!" said Des. "Humans will believe anything! Right, your parents are getting a bit suspicious about the quiet down here, so perhaps you'd better head upstairs and make a bit of noise. Don't overdo it. I'll check outside to make sure they've gone and left no trace. See you later. How did you get out, by the way – and how did they get in?"

Ollie explained, and showed the hidden passage, while the others made their way upstairs. "But don't tell the parents about this door, Des. Please! We have to get out on our own sometimes!"

Des gave him a hard stare. "Did I hear you mutter something about '*getting old*'...?"

"Didn't mean *you*, obviously...."

"Good thing! Now scram!" He gave Ollie a cheerful buffet with one wing and grinned happily as he took off over the fence to search for traces of the invaders. He was beginning to think that Ollie might make a good travelling mate...

Upstairs, the others took deep calming breaths as they entered the kitchen, but fortunately their plea for drinks seemed quite normal, and nobody looked suspicious. Duncan, sitting by the fire, was looking a lot better, Emily thought. He glanced at the ball that Tom was still clutching. "What's that?" he asked.

"Tennis ball. Humans left it in a room upstairs. There's some more of their rubbish and stuff too, but I brought this down for Tail-Stane in the hall. Want a game?"

"What did you call it?" asked Gwen.

"I think that's what it is," said Emily hurriedly. "I read about it in a book."

"Much better than a stone for inside," Tom was saying as he left the kitchen with his father and Oliver. Ollie gulped more water and followed them out. "Mind your wing!" Gwen called after Duncan, shaking her head.

"What have you girls got round your arms?" Ellen asked casually.

"Not sure," said Alice. "We found them upstairs in the room where the balls were."

"Quite pretty," said Ellen. "You'll be rivalling your aunt at this rate!"

"But please don't search for perfume," added George. "One heavily scented dragon is quite enough!"

A burst of cheering from the hall gave them an excuse to hurry out. They looked at one another and grinned. "Quick thinking!" said Emily.

The racket in the hall was soon explained. Des had joined the game. "Coming on my team?" he asked, aiming the ball over Ollie's head at Tom, who jumped and bounced it off his head instead of his tail. Alice and Emily shook their heads and retreated to the room across the passage. They felt like curling up together on Angie's couch and discussing the amazing events of the afternoon in peace and quiet.

"I wish I'd had something to give Emily and Alice like you did," Megan whispered to Lisa as they hurried home through the snow.

"Perhaps you can!" said Lisa. "There's a bag of books waiting for the next jumble sale in your spare room. Let's see if there's any they might like. Nobody would know if we crept round and shoved them through the hole in the fence. We can cover our tracks. I know they'd LOVE some new books! What do you think?"

Megan beamed. "Can I choose? I think I know which ones they'd like best!" she said happily.

She was right. Alice and Emily were delighted when they found their present two days later, and the addition of a battered black and white football in a bag was enough to keep the boys happy.

"How do we explain these away?" Ollie asked, obviously tempted.

"We found them in the room upstairs of course!" chorused the girls.

"That big cupboard we broke open is obviously FULL of old junk!" Emily added. "Enough to keep us going for the rest of the winter!"

END OF BOOK V

Appendix 1:
My Memories of Snow

A good deal of "Dragons in Snow" is based on family memories of past winters, which (of course) were MUCH colder and more snowy than the winters we have now.....

Long, long ago, in the last century – the late 1970s and 80s – in the Lammermuir Hills in East Lothian where we lived, we had some VERY snowy winters.

In the garden, over the years my children were growing up, there were igloos big enough for several to sit inside, snow caves you could hide in, a drift covering the greenhouse, and rabbits and hares that hopped over the buried fences to nibble bark off the branches of the fruit trees. There was a wee pony who would pull a sledge, once a make-shift harness of long scarves and rope had been invented.

The sledge in question was built by Grandpa, my father. It was large and solidly built of wood, painted orange and *extremely* heavy. It took many passengers, but nobody ever volunteered to pull it back up the hill. Thick plastic bags proved more popular, and good for bob-sleigh runs. (I don't think plastic sledges had been invented.)

School buses didn't run for weeks. Nobody at my school on the coast believed that I couldn't get to work until I showed the photo of our front door hidden behind its drift. A visitor's car had to be abandoned where it had stuck, and spent three weeks inside a snowdrift.

In 1984 the snow was so deep that the roads disappeared under drifts that stretched between the dry-stone walls and they had to bring JCB diggers (yellow dragons!) and a snow-blower as it was too deep for the snow ploughs. We had five days without electricity, and supplies had to be fetched by sledge.

We learned that even if no fresh snow is falling, just a small shift in the wind direction will blow all the loose snow into new drifts, cover all the paths you have just finished digging out and block the roads – again. We learned how dangerous a blizzard can be, and that you can get lost very close to home, when you have to abandon the car and continue on foot.

So this book is for Kate, Martin, Rachel and all the friends who came to enjoy the snow with them over the years; especially Mike, cycling from the civilised city, who carried his bike over the drifts for the last mile or so, and the many stranded waifs and strays who slept on floors.

Peter and I still live in the house on the north-facing slope of the Lammermuirs, and 'proper' snow still happens occasionally. On Christmas Day 2011, my mother, aged 95, was carried in her wheelchair up the snowy steps to the front door by four of her grandchildren, to be met by dancing great-grandchildren in the hall. There was no way she was missing Christmas with the family, whatever Health and Safety decreed. "It might be my last!" she said. "No it won't!" said the children, and they were right.

There was a memorable Easter Sunday in 2013. After Sunday Dinner for fourteen in a local pub, we had three generations of bag-sliders on snowy slopes, an improvised 'ski-jump' over a covered wood-pile and lots of snowball battles, all beneath a bright blue sky.

Today I am looking out at snow again. It's not as deep as it used to be, but my grandchildren and their friends are enjoying it, and on the hillside there is a a Fort with a tunnel through it (built by David with Seamus and Tom) and a wonderful 5 foot sculpture of a Snow Bear (created by Elise and Eleanor). I go out to admire them, before I put the kettle on for hot drinks....

Judy Hayman

January 15th 2016

Appendix 2: Glossary

A short glossary of some of the Scots language, as used by the Otter family and the Buzzards in this book, the Bonxie in *Quest for Adventure* and some of the Hawks in *The Runaway*.

Hint: If you are puzzled by the spelling of a word, try reading it aloud as it is written. You will often guess what it means. Some of the words below are easy to guess, but some are more unusual and have special meanings.

Afore: before

Anither: another

Back th' noo: back in a minute

Bairns: children

Bidin': living

Birled: whirled

Blaeberries: the Scots name for blueberries (or bilberries or whinberries in different parts of England.)

Bonxie: Great Skua – a large fierce seabird

Braw: nice, good, lovely – general approval!

Coorie doon: snuggle up (or down)

Daein': doing

Deid: dead

Dinnae: don't

Dinnae fash: don't worry

Dreich: dark, drizzly, miserable weather (wonderful Scots word to describe a wet Highland day!)

Drookit: soaked with water, bedraggled (another good one!)

Dugs: dogs

Feart: frightened

Frae: from

Gae: Go

Geme: game

Gloaming: evening, twilight or dusk (very important for dragons because it's the time of the Gloaming Huff)

Guddle: muddle

Hae a shot: have a go, try it

Heid: head, or chief

Isnae: isn't

Keek : look

Ken: know ('ye ken' is used exactly like 'you know')

Loch: a freshwater lake, like the one near the Dragons' cave (a little one is a 'lochan')

Mair: more

Micht: might

Mingin': disgusting

Nae: No

Naebdy: nobody

Nae danger: no problem or no chance

Nicht: night

Onyways: anyway

Selkies: seals (there are a lot of lovely old tales about Selkies told in Scotland)

Ta'en: taken

Tatties: potatoes – usually pronounced without the middle 't's

Telt: told

Thirz: there is or there are

Wilnae: won't

Yez: you – usually plural

Yin: one

Yince: once

Acknowledgements

Thanks as ever to Caroline and Alison, for continuing to fit the illustrating and publishing of these stories into their increasingly frenetic lives. What would I do without you?

Again thanks to my grandchildren! It was Phoebe's idea to get Ben McIlwhinnie up and walking; Sam's passion for football inspired the Tail-Stane game; Megan supplied some of the chapter headings, and she and Elise (Lisa) lent their names. I still have David's Big Idea to use in Book VI.

Peter, as always, provides admin support and emergency technical help as we ease along my aged computer. Gordon helped with the glossary and Martin added to my snow memories. George told me about Silverweed roots and gave me other foraging tips. Sylvia expanded my school contacts.

Rachel's marketing skills are much appreciated. Kate and her colleagues in Stirling, and Gill in Haydon Bridge, have arranged lovely school visits and introduced the dragons to new readers. Thanks to those who have sent me reviews and pictures. I cherish the memory of the red squirrels in the playground of Strathyre, the School in the Glen; and am delighted with the enthusiasm for reading and writing that I have found in all the schools I have visited. Thank you, teachers – you're doing a great job!

About the Author

 Judy Hayman lives with her husband Peter on the edge of the Lammermuir Hills in East Lothian, Scotland, where there is a wonderful view and plenty of wildlife, but no dragons, as far as she knows. At various times in her past life she has taught English in a big comprehensive school; written plays, directed and occasionally acted for amateur theatre companies; been a Parliamentary candidate for both Westminster and the Scottish Parliament; and a Mum. Sometimes all at once. Now preventing the Lammermuirs from taking over her garden, being a Gran, writing more Dragon Tales and visiting schools to talk about them takes up a lot of her time.

About the Illustrator

 Caroline Wolfe Murray studied Archaeology at the University of Edinburgh and took a career path in the field, turning her hand to archaeological illustration. She has always had a passion for exploration and discovery which evolved from her experience of living in Spain, Belgium, Venezuela and New Zealand. She now resides in East Lothian with her husband James and her two young daughters Lily and Mabel, who have been her inspiration to work on a children's book.

Spring is coming, the snow is melting and the young dragons are growing up. Soon it will be time to leave the castle and head home to Ben McIlwhinnie and their Scottish Glen.

Being trapped in the castle leads to quarrels and new alliances, a desperate hunt, and help from unexpected friends. There is excitement and sorrow too.

There are many challenges for Emily and Tom and their family and friends to face.

Find out more in *Dragon Tales Book VI: The Dragons' Call* by Judy Hayman, coming soon.

NOW AVAILABLE: The Dragon Tales Colouring Book

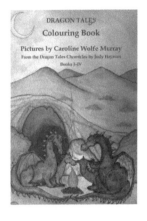

A selection of Caroline Wolfe Murray's lovely illustrations enlarged for you to colour and keep.

40 pages of beautiful pictures, with information about the Dragons and their adventures. For more information on the Dragon Tales books, email info@alisonjones.com.

Read on for the first chapter of Dragon Tales Book VI: The Dragons' Call, *coming soon...*

Chapter 1

Spring on the Way

A loud yell from Tom made everybody jump. Emily, Alice and Ollie, who had been looking out of the other three windows of the Tower room in Aunt Angelica's Castle, looked round, startled. Des, sorting his travelling bundle in the middle of his untidy hay bed, even leapt to his feet. Then they all began to laugh. Tom had leaned too far out of his window, and a huge dollop of melting snow had fallen from the roof onto his head, covering one eye and lodging itself onto his bright blue spikes.

"Idiot!" said Ollie.

"Don't shake your head!" said Emily, but it was too late. A vigorous shake from Tom sent drips of wet snow flying across the room. Des growled as the largest dollop landed on his bed.

"Why are you all lurking up here anyway?" he complained. "We know the snow's melting at last. There's no need to watch it happen!" He gave a suspicious glare round the four young dragons. "I don't suppose you're watching out for those little Human friends of yours, are you?"

Emily and Alice assumed expressions of innocence, but Ollie scowled. "They're no friends of mine!" he declared.

"Huh, you like playing with that ball they gave you as much as Tom does," Alice said, making Ollie scowl even more. "And we're NOT looking for them, Des. There's been no sign of them. They promised to leave us alone, and they *have* done. You're far too suspicious. Typical grown-up! Come on, Emily – let's go out."

She flounced out of the room with her nose in the air, and Emily followed, flashing Des an apologetic glance as she went. Tom tried to stay behind, but a determined shove from Ollie sent him out after the girls, and the battered door was firmly shut behind him. He sighed and trailed slowly down the stairs as Alice and Emily squeezed through the hole in the huge front door, and disappeared into the garden.

He headed for the kitchen. Maggie might feel sorry for him left on his own, and find him a snack.

Out in the garden, Emily and Alice headed for their favourite place. It was a flat branch growing sideways out of the trunk of an ash tree at the edge of the garden. The trees of the wood grew thickly behind it on the other side of the boundary fence, so there was little chance of being spotted from outside. Fortunately they were mainly fir trees, so even in winter the dragons were well hidden. They flew up, settled side by side facing the Castle and hoped that nobody would disturb them.

"When the leaves come out we'll be completely hidden up here," said Alice.

Emily looked at her, puzzled. "We won't be here then," she said. "Dad's wing is nearly better. As soon as the snow's completely gone, and he's strong enough, we'll be heading home to our cave. And you're coming too, aren't you?"

"I hope so," said Alice. "But it will depend on what the parents decide. I think they quite like living here, even with old Ange. It's better for Grandad." She sighed heavily, and Emily decided to change the subject.

"I *was* looking out for Lisa and the others," she admitted. "I know we said we wouldn't, but I'd LOVE to see them again, wouldn't you?"

The young dragons had had a fright a few weeks previously, at the height of the snowy winter, when four Human children had discovered their secret hide-out in the old ruined house that was Alice's Aunt Angelica's home. The winter had been so severe that she had invited all her family to join her in her 'castle', and had taken in Emily's family too, when their cave had been blocked with snow. There was plenty of room for them all, but Emily knew that as soon as her father's broken wing had healed, he would want to return home to their cave in the

Scottish glen. And she wanted to go home herself – but she wanted her friends to come too!

"I knew they'd keep their promise," Alice said. "There's been no sign of any other Human in the woods, so they can't have told anybody else about us. And Des blocked up the hole in the fence, so they couldn't get back in, even if they sneaked back this way themselves. I'm glad the parents never found out, though."

"It was nice of them to give us those books," Emily said. "I wish I could have said thank you!" She twiddled the coloured bobble on her arm, looked at the blue one that Alice wore, the token of friendship that Lisa had given them, and decided to confess. "I'd love to sneak out and get a proper look at the place they live in! Wouldn't you?"

Alice, who was a little older and a good deal more sensible, looked at her severely. "Don't even DREAM about it!" she said. "Forget them. It was great, but it's finished. We were lucky only Des found out. Stop talking about them. It's chilly out here. Let's see if it's supper time."

They flew down from the branch and across to the front door, over patches of bright green that were appearing as the snow gradually melted. There were still deep drifts in many places, and the clouds were low in the sky, threatening rain. Winter was departing, but the outside world was not inviting, and the young dragons were still confined to the tangled garden of the old house, inside the high fence. Sighing for the summer and the wide open spaces of her beloved Scottish glen, Emily followed Alice inside.

Meanwhile, up in the Tower room, Ollie had taken advantage of having Des to himself, and was using his most persuasive tactics. The sight of Des sorting his travelling gear had made him realise that it would not be long before Des's itchy wings got the better of him, and he set off on his travels again. As Des himself had said several times recently, he had never stayed so long in one place since he was a youngster.

"I have to get going again, Ollie," he was arguing. "I'm a Traveller. I'm getting fat on all this good cooking. Not enough exercise. I can't stay here forever."

"Neither can I!" said Ollie. "OK, it was good of old Ange to take us in, and we couldn't have camped out this winter, but I'll go MAD if I have to stay in this place for much longer. Winter's just about over. Can't I come with you? Honestly, I am old enough! You wouldn't have to protect me, or anything stupid like that. I can fly fast and keep going. Why not?"

"Are you sure you've got over that fright in the summer, when the Humans captured you?" Des stared seriously at Ollie. "That was enough to panic any dragon."

"Course I have!" Ollie lied, crossing his tail, and not admitting that he still dreamt about his ordeal and woke in the night, sweating and terrified. It was a good thing Tom, who shared his cellar room, was such a sound sleeper! He changed his tactics. "You've got to admit I did a good job of getting rid of those Human kids. And they haven't been back, so I must have REALLY scared them."

"True. Though I seem to remember I helped!"

"PLEASE, Des! I'm sure Dad will agree if you ask him, and then we can talk Mum round. Old Ange would be glad to see the back of me. She wants *you* to stay, though," he added, sniggering. Angelica's persistent flirting was a source of great embarrassment to Des and amusement to everyone else.

Des ignored this. "I'll think about it. I was planning to take a short trip to get my wings in trim, then to come back here to pick up Duncan and Gwen for the trip north. See them all safe to their cave. Duncan's not quite ready for such a long flight yet, but I know he's longing to get back to the glen. He may need to take it slowly with his mended wing, and he won't be up to giving Tom a lift if he needs one."

Ollie beamed. "Short trip, just us two! Sounds perfect for a start. Where shall we go?"

"I haven't said yes! It'll be hard on Tom if you take off."

Ollie scowled. "He's OK, but he's just a kid. I can't be expected to stay and look after him. You'll be expecting me to babysit Georgie and Lily next!"

Des laughed at the thought, and clapped Ollie with one wing. "OK, I will think about it, I promise. But only if your parents agree. I'm not having you sneaking off again, even with me. Once was enough!"

A call from below brought the discussion to an end, and they headed down for food. As far as Ollie was concerned, the matter was decided. He couldn't wait to tell the others!

For more information on the Dragon Tales books, email info@alisonjones.com.

THE DRAGON TALES CHRONICLES

Book I: Quest for a Cave

Book II: Quest for a Friend

Book III: Quest for Adventure

Book IV: The Runaway

Book V: Dragons in Snow

Book VI: The Dragons' Call *(due for publication November 2016)*

For more information on the Dragon Tales books,
email info@alisonjones.com.

The Scottish Dragon Family

They live in a cave in a remote Highland glen, well away from dangerous Humans.

Emily	Tom	Lily
Imaginative and adventurous	Young brother, lively	The baby, born in Book II
Purply-blue with lighter wings	Bright blue	Gold – very rare

Their Parents	
Gwen	**Duncan**
Unusual turquoise blue	Dark blue

Their Grandparents, who live in Wales and come to visit in Book III	
Nan	**Edward**
Green	Dark blue, but with touches of gold on spikes and wing

The English Dragon Family

They first appear in Book II, and are various shades of red, pink and orange. They travel around the country, camping in secret places, well hidden from Humans. Aunt Angelica, who turns up in Book IV, thinks herself very grand because she lives in a 'castle'.

Ollie	Alice	Georgie
Eldest, wild and reckless	Sensible and thoughtful	Small and bouncy
Tom's hero	Emily's friend	

Their Parents	Their Grandfather	Their Aunt
Ellen and Oliver	Old George	Angelica, or Angie